JOHNNY BALL
ACCIDENTAL FOOTBALL GENIUS

MATT OLDFIELD

ILLUSTRATED BY TIM WESSON

WALKER
BOOKS

CHAPTER 1

THE BALLS: A FOOTBALL FAMILY

If I had to pick three words to describe my family,
I'd go for:

1.   FOOTBALL
2.   **FOOTBALL**

and...

3.   **FOOTBALL.**

Dad

Daniel

Mum

me
(Johnny)

"What else is there?" my dad likes to say. He also likes to say that if he hadn't broken his right ankle playing for Tissbury Town when he was younger, he would have been a football superstar. "I'd have won the World Cup for sure!" he says often. I used to think this was a joke, but he never laughs when he says it.

Whenever Dad talks about his right ankle, Mum rolls her eyes and stops listening. She does that when I tell her my most horrible jokes too.

"Why was Tigger in the toilet?"

"I don't know."

"Because he was looking for Pooh!"

"Urgh, DISGUSTING!"

Mum used to be the captain of Tissbury Town Ladies, but she never boasts about being so good.

Tissbury Town is our local football club. We go to watch their games every weekend at the Railway Road Stadium. My older brother, Daniel, already plays for their youth team, the Tissbury Tigers Under-15s. He's a speedy striker and, according to Dad, one of the best young players that our town has ever seen. I think Dad might be right about that one, for once.

And what about me? Well, I was named after two Tissbury Town legends:

BURY TIMES ✠

JOHNNY "THE ROCKET" JEFFRIES

Tissbury's all-time top scorer with 911 goals.

✠ TISSBURY TIM

NIGEL "HARD HANDS" ANDREWS

Tissbury's Number One until he was 43 years old. He was so good in goal that he didn't even wear gloves!

But don't worry about all that – just call me Johnny. Nice to meet you!

Luckily, I love football just as much as my mum, dad and brother do. I love football for lots and lots of reasons: the action, the excitement, even the offside rule. When a bunch of people kick a ball around a pitch, you just never know what's going to happen next, do you?

I love reading about football,

I love looking at pictures of football,

I love collecting stickers about football,

I love talking about football,

I love listening to other people talk about football (even my dad!),

I love watching football

and I love playing football.

If I didn't, life would be really hard in my family! Who would I talk to?

You're probably thinking, "Great, so what's your problem?"

Well, unfortunately, I'M NOT THAT GOOD AT FOOTBALL. There, I've said it!

I'm not saying I'm terrible at football. No, I'm a whole lot better than some kids I know – not naming names *COUGH* Sammy Sharples *COUGH* – but I'm never going to be the next Johnny "The Rocket" Jeffries, or the next Daniel "The Cannon" Ball. Sadly, the fact that I really love football isn't enough to give me special powers on the pitch.

I'll tell you a secret: it used to get me down a little. But now things have changed. My whole world has changed, and that's why I'm telling you my story. Trust me – it's a story worth hearing!

Right, that's enough of a warm-up. It's time for kick-off...

CHAPTER 2

BILLY THE BULLY

It all started on a super-normal Monday morning.
I was just doing what I always do: kicking a stone
to school and pretending I was "The Rocket".
Suddenly, I heard a big, bellowing voice behind me.

OI, JOHNNY!

Uh-oh! I didn't
even need to
turn around.
I already
knew who
it was:
Billy, or
"Billy the
Bully" as
I usually
call him.

Billy Newland has been making my life a misery ever since I started nursery. He's in the year above me now, but back then, when we had to play together, he used to steal my toys and kick my sandcastles. Now that he can walk and talk (well, sort of...), he's even more of a bully.

What did he want this time? I tried my best to ignore him, but that never works with Billy. When he has something to bellow, he doesn't stop until everyone hears it.

"Oi, Johnny, I'm talking to you!"

"S-sorry, I, err, didn't hear you." (Yeah, I'm a rubbish liar.)

"Whatever, I wanted to ask you something. What's your middle name?"

As Billy said it, he nudged Alex C next to him, the stupidest of his sidekicks. Billy always has to have an audience.

Double uh-oh! How did he know my secret? You see, I don't mind the Johnny – there are millions of boys called Johnny – but Nigel? How many boys do you know with that name? I bet I know the answer: ZERO! No one needed to know about the Nigel, and especially not Billy. Someone must have told him – but who? Daniel? Tabia? They were the only two who knew my secret.

"It's err..."

Think, Johnny, think! When I'm watching football, I have lots of great ideas (I'll tell you more about them later), but when I'm walking to school on a Monday morning? Not so much.

"...N-Neil."

"Really? Because I heard your middle name was Johnny 'CAN'T KICK THE' Ball!"

"No, it isn't!" I wanted to shout back but, of course, I didn't. I was just super relieved that he didn't know about the Nigel.

"Good one, mate!" Alex C grunted like a pig with its snout still in the trough.

As if that was even funny. Billy thinks he's the funniest person on Planet Earth, but he's really not. He tells the same jokes so many times that they're not just old, they're as ANCIENT as the pyramids of Egypt!

JOHNNY CAN'T KICK THE BALL! HA, HA, HA!

The worst part is that everyone in the Tissbury Primary School playground laughs at my name every time. They don't do it because it's funny. They do it because they're too scared not to. Billy is the biggest kid in Year 6 and he makes sure everyone knows it.

It's the same with football. Billy walks around our school playground like he owns it, wearing the latest Tissbury Town kit and a pair of gleaming gold boots. But he doesn't even own the ball – it's Mo's!

Anyway, every lunchtime, Billy is:

the referee,

the captain,

the coach

and the penalty-taker.

It's like there's a school rule that says:

BILLY NEWLAND MUST NEVER LOSE A FOOTBALL MATCH.

And he isn't just annoying in the playground; no, even on my morning walk to school, Billy was there, making my life a misery.

Once they'd eventually stopped laughing at that terrible joke, I thought they would just barge straight past and leave me alone. That's what Billy usually does. But, no, he wasn't finished yet.

"Oi, Johnny, you're not coming to the County Cup team trial tomorrow, are you?" he bellowed, even though I was standing right beside him. "Don't bother; you'll NEVER make it! Shame you didn't get your brother's skills!"

And with that, Billy and Alex C FINALLY swaggered off to school, snorting and snuffling like farmyard beasts.

Let me explain. In Years 5 and 6, the Tissbury Primary football team becomes a REALLY BIG DEAL. The Under-11s County Cup is all anyone talks about. Who should be in the team, who should be out of the team, who should be captain … it goes on and on and on. Imagine the World Cup, but just for our local area. Actually, forget the word "just" – the County Cup is SUPER HUGE!

Every year, our school gets really excited, but we've only won the Cup twice in the last twenty years. And even that was only because Daniel scored all of Tissbury Primary's goals.

Now that I was in Year 5, it was my chance to follow in my brother's brilliant stud marks. Winning the County Cup was a moment that I had dreamed about for years. When I closed my eyes at night, I could picture the party, the pride, the glory, the winners' medal and, of course, that glittering trophy…

But now that Billy was in Year 6, did that mean he would be captain of the Tissbury Primary team? If so, he was right; I would NEVER make it.

According to Billy, he's the best player ever. That's because he thinks football is all about power. His left foot is fiercer than a mighty pirate cannon. Billy "The Blaster" Newland – that's the nickname that he gave himself in Year 4. It didn't really catch on, though, despite him having it written on the back of his Tissbury Town shirt.

If Billy really HOOFs! the ball, it flies all the way from one end of the pitch to the other. It's best to get out of the way, unless you want to be in loads of pain and have a big, red, football-shaped tattoo. He's such a kicking king that the ball makes a special sound when he kicks it: *CLANK!*

Forget footwork or tactics. If you can't boot the ball really far, Billy thinks you're rubbish at football.

Well, who cares what he thinks? brave me argued with the less brave me inside my brain as I walked through the playground. *Billy knows nothing about PROPER football! If I want to get on the Tissbury Primary team and win the County Cup, then that's what I'm going to do. I'm not going to let anyone stop me, especially not a big bully like him.*

At the trials, I was just going to have to show him by playing the best football of my life.

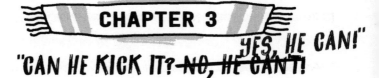

CHAPTER 3

"CAN HE KICK IT? ~~NO, HE CAN'T!~~ YES, HE CAN!"

As you can tell, I'm not Billy's number one fan. The thing that annoys me most is that he's a big fat liar. I CAN KICK THE BALL!

When I was seven, I even scored a hat-trick for the Tissbury Tiger Cubs. Yeah, take that, Billy the Bully!

The problem was that, two years later, that was still my most glorious football achievement. I try my hardest on the pitch but I'm not:

the tallest,

or the strongest,

or the quickest,

or the bravest.

I'm good, but I'm just not Johnny "The Rocket" Jeffries good, or Daniel "The Cannon" Ball good either.

To make things worse, my football career was at a dead end. I was now too old to play for the Tiger

Cubs and not quite good enough to be selected for the Tigers Under-11s. So, what was I supposed to do now? Other than going to see Tissbury Town play at the Railway Road Stadium, weekends were suddenly super boring. Either I went along with Mum and Dad to watch Daniel being brilliant at what I wished I could do, or I sat at home feeling sorry for myself. That's like choosing between eating brains or eyes for breakfast. Yuck!

"We can't be superstars at everything, cutie-pie!" Mum told me pretty much every Saturday morning as Daniel left for practice, with a sad "I wish I could give you some of my skills" smile.

Sometimes, I felt like I was letting my football family down. After all, over the years, they'd done everything they could to help me become a better player.

It started when I was four years old. One day, I was watching TV on a Saturday morning when Dad walked in with a football tucked under his arm.

"Right, son, it's time to start your training!" he said, like a soldier about to set out on a very important mission. I was super excited.

In the back garden, Dad dropped the ball down and swung his leg slowly to show me how to kick it.

"Like THIS – owwwww, my ankle!"

It was my turn next, my big football debut. I clenched my fists, shut my eyes and swung my little right leg as hard as I could. **BANG!**

I opened my eyes, expecting to see the ball shooting through the air at the speed of light. But instead, it was inching across the grass at the speed of a snail!

"Not bad," was all Dad said. Not bad, but not that good either. He kept trying to teach me, but I didn't really get much better.

Then once I turned six, I started playing for the Tiger Cubs. After the high of that one-and-only hat-trick I've already told you about, I quickly came crashing back down to earth. I missed a super-easy shot in the next match and shuffled through the front door looking like the saddest saddo in Sadville. That's when I discovered that Mum was a much better football coach than Dad.

"Never mind, poppet," she said, taking a football off the shelf (yes, in our house, we have a whole shelf just for footballs). "With a bit more practice, we'll have you scoring again in no time!"

"Ready?" Mum called, already outside in the garden. Apparently, that practice had to begin straight away. She crossed the ball in, and I kicked it past the imaginary keeper (oh yeah, we have a goal in our back garden too).

"Good, that's better!" Mum clapped. "See, you can do it – calm and steady scores the goal!" She had an encouraging phrase for everything.

Sure, but that was just a tap-in into an empty net. What about when there was actually someone there to save it? After a few more goals, Mum went inside to grab her keeper gloves (different shelf, obviously).

"Give me your best shot, buddy!" she shouted, putting on her awful American accent. She even pointed her fingers like they were cowboy guns. Super embarrassing!

But I was ready for this. I clenched my fists, swung my leg as hard as I could, and **BANG!**

I expected to see the ball sailing towards the top corner of the net. But instead, it went sailing over the fence and we heard it **PLOP** down into Mrs Taylor's pond.

"Sorry!" Mum and I both yelled, running back inside before she could shout at us. Sadly, that was the end of our garden games. Even Mum is scared of Mrs Taylor, you see.

Over the years, Daniel and I have kicked so many balls over Mrs Taylor's fence and not a single one has ever come back. We're too frightened to look, but her garden must be like a football graveyard by now!

Anyway, speaking of my big brother, he helped me a lot too. Until Daniel left Tissbury Primary, we used to go to Parsley Park together for a kick-around almost every weekend. And during that summer holiday before he started at Tissbury High, we went there every single day. One day, he came up with a fun new game for us to play.

He called it "Rainbow". It started with short passes to each other, but soon they were getting longer and longer and higher and higher, until we were almost at opposite sides of the park. The Ball Brothers were putting on a real football show!

I was having so much fun that I wasn't even thinking any more. It was just one touch to control and then **BANG!**

The ball was supposed to land at Daniel's feet, just like all my other passes. But instead, the ball zoomed through the air, over Daniel's head, and bounced right off a dog's nose! He wasn't a cute little puppy either; he was the biggest, meanest dog I'd ever seen, and he was off the lead.

"Grrrrrrrrrrrr!" Long strings of drool were hanging from his mouth. He eyed me up like I was his next meal, before tearing into the ball.

"Oi!" his owner added. He looked a lot like his dog.

"Sorry!" I shouted.

Daniel refused to play football with me in public after that. As I said earlier, I'm good at football, but I'm not THAT good.

I guess that's why the County Cup team trial meant so much to me. It wouldn't be easy, but I had to try. This was my big chance to find a new team, and hopefully make my family proud. I was a Ball, after all. So, if I was going to be a superstar at something, it had to be football!

CHAPTER 4

THE COUNTY CUP TEAM TRIAL

Mum had added "JOHNNY'S TEAM TRIAL!!!" on the family football calendar months ago, but I'd cleverly covered it up with a Tissbury Town sticker. I didn't need the extra pressure of a "Good Luck!" and a "Go do us proud!". All I wanted was the "Well Done!" once it was all over and I had (hopefully) made the team. So, I just ate my breakfast quietly, like it was another normal Tuesday...

I really didn't want to bump into Billy again, so I walked to school with Tabia instead. She lives one street away and she's the best kind of best friend: funny, smart and as brave as a lion and a bull combined. Even Billy is a bit scared of Tabs! That's mainly because she's really good at nasty name battles. It's one of our favourite things to do.

"So, are you ready for the team trial today, **_NOODLE-NECK?_**"

"Of course, **FERRET-FACE!**"

"You'd better be, **BOGEY-BRAIN!**"

Tabs was the winner ... again.

"OK, but seriously," she said. "Are you feeling nervous?"

"Not really," I lied. The truth was it felt like frogs were fighting a pirate war in my tummy.

I was so desperate to do well in the trial, but I couldn't tell Tabs that, could I?

Instead, I said, "Billy reckons I've got no chance."

Tabia rolled her eyes. "Who cares what he thinks? You've got to believe in yourself, **SEA-SQUIRT!** Trust me, you and I are going to win the County Cup together. You'll see!"

It was easy for her to say that; Tabia is one of the best footballers in Tissbury. She's got MAD SKILLZ. At first, the boys didn't let her play with them, but eventually they gave in. They probably regret that now because she runs rings around all of them!

Billy always picks her for his team.

People in Tissbury think she'll even play for England one day. "Girl's got game!" my mum likes to say in her awful American accent. I've told her to stop so many times, but she's unstoppable. Sometimes, Tabia comes round for kick-abouts in our garden, but not with me, with my mum instead! How embarrassing is that?

Anyway, let's get to the main event. That day, the clock in our classroom seemed to move in slow motion, but eventually the school day ended, and sixteen boys and girls raced out onto the pitch to get warmed up for the trial.

There were good things and bad things about playing for the Tissbury Primary team. The good thing was that Billy wasn't in charge of everything! Tissbury Primary had their own proper football coach. Well, sort of, and that's where the bad things began...

"RIGHT, TROOPS," Mr Mann boomed, rolling up the sleeves of his tracksuit to show his seriously huge and hairy arms. It was the first time I had ever seen him up close. Everything about Mr Mann was massive:

the loud voice,

the enormous egghead,

the bulging biceps,

the thunder thighs

and the great big belly.

He looked like he
might pop at any
moment, like one of
those balloon animals
that clowns make at
birthday parties.

"LET'S GET STARTED!
I WANT YOU TO LEAVE
EVERYTHING ON THE PITCH
TODAY!"

What – even our
football kit?

Uh-oh, we had a
problem. It turned out that Mr Mann only spoke the
language of silly football people.

Why can't football people just say normal things
that make sense? That's one of the things I like most
about Tabia. She's a super-awesome footballer
who scores loads of goals, but you won't catch her

calling them "HOWLERS" and "SCREAMERS", as if the ball can talk.

We didn't practise any passing, or dribbling, or shooting or tackling. No, Mr Mann just threw some bibs at us and then watched as we played a big match. His instructions were so confusing:

MAN ON!

Man on what? Man on the pitch? Man on the moon?

BURY IT!   **CUSHION IT!**

PUT IT IN THE MIXER!

DON'T BOTTLE IT!

That was a lot of different things to do and not do to "it"!

The game was more like a talent show than a team sport. One by one, the players showed off as many skills as they could before someone else stole the ball.

I'll be honest with you. It wasn't the best game of football I've ever played either. In fact, it was one of the worst. It was almost as bad as that time I missed a super-easy shot for the Tissbury Tiger Cubs.

Sorry, I promise I'll stop mentioning that match...

There was a lot of punting and not much passing, but Mr Mann didn't seem to mind. In fact, the only time he clapped was when Billy HOOFed! it all the way from one end of the pitch to the other. **CLANK!**

THAT'S IT – SHOW THAT BALL WHO'S BOSS!

Really, was that the game plan? After that, the Year 6 kids just kicked it long to each other, while us Year 5s scrambled around trying to get near the ball. It was more like tennis than football!

I'd barely had a touch all game. How was I meant to prove Billy wrong and show that I could kick a ball? Playing in the County Cup had always been my dream, but I could feel it slipping further and further away. I had to do something before it reached outer space!

I wasn't the only one who wasn't enjoying the trial. Tabia was on my team and her frown was so deep you could drown in it.

"At this rate, I won't even make the bench!" she moaned during the drinks break. "Scott isn't falling for any of my MAD SKILLZ. It's like that *LIZARD-LIPS* can read my mind or something. I don't know what to do, Johnny. I need to score! Help, I need one of your football ideas!"

Oh wait, I haven't told you about those yet, have I? Sorry! I might not have great football SKILLZ, but I do have great football IDEAS. When I'm watching football, I sometimes have these moments when it's like a light bulb flicks on in my brain. When that happens, it only means one thing: a great football idea! At school, I usually keep them to myself, especially if Billy's around, but Tabia was my best friend and she needed one NOW. So, I searched and searched my football brain, until at last...

TING! LIGHT-BULB MOMENT!

"Scott's a good defender, but he's got a really sweet tooth. Try this," I said and then I whispered my idea to her.

Scott was a long way away, but still, if you've got a really clever plan, you should always whisper it, just in case. It makes the whole thing way more exciting.

"Cool, thanks, it's worth a try!" Tabia said as we ran back onto the field.

I don't mean to boast like Billy, but that idea was my greatest football idea EVER! The next time Tabia got the ball, she showed off her MAD SKILLZ as usual – stepover 1, stepover 2, stepover 3, stepover 4 – but again, her fancy feet weren't fooling Scott. It was time for the masterplan.

"Look!" She pointed off the pitch. "What's Mr Flake's ice-cream van doing here? It's October!"

"Where?" Scott replied, turning his head like those meerkats on TV.

NUTMEG!

Tabia tapped the ball through his legs and scored top bins.

GOOOOOOOOAAAAAAALLLL!

Usually, when one of us does something great (like acing one of Miss Patel's spelling tests, or doing a really long, loud burp), Tabia and I celebrate with our special secret handshake (no, I can't describe it – it's SECRET). We'd spent hours making it super awesome, but it could wait until after the team trial. Instead, Tabia just looked at me and gave me a quick thumbs up that said:

JOHNNY BALL, YOU'RE A FOOTBALL GENIUS!

I gave a quick thumbs up back and that made Billy even angrier than the goal had. Not only was his team losing, but my team was also winning.

"What are you smiling about?" he snarled at me. He looked like a big sweaty bull dressed in football kit. "Who do you think you are, Johnny – your brother? Ha, as if! Just watch it, or I'll give another BALL a good kicking!"

I thought that was just a stupid threat, but no. Before I could react, Billy HOOFed! the ball as hard as he could. *CLANK!* It was hurtling towards me at top speed, and not towards my right foot, or my left foot. It was about to hit me right in the … face.

SMACK!

"Owwwww!" I cried out as I lay sprawled on the grass. It felt like I'd been hit by a bus, not a ball. My ears were ringing.

"Whoops! Sorry," Billy shouted without even trying to hide his big grin. "I was just doing what Mr Mann told me to do – showing that BALL who's boss!"

Brilliant, my team trial was over, and that meant so was my dream of playing in the County Cup. And just as I had thought, it was all because of Billy. Nooooooo! There would be no party, no pride, no glory, no winners' medal, no glittering trophy, NO NOTHING!

I trudged off to get an ice pack from the school office and then went straight home before Billy the Bully could make any more jokes. I was so upset that I didn't kick a single stone along the way. It felt like my football career was over.

My football family were going to be so disappointed. In fact, maybe I just wouldn't tell them. It wasn't on the calendar, so hopefully they'd have just forgotten…

🏆 🏆 🏆

The next day, we had to wait until lunchtime before Mr Mann put up the list outside his office. Of the sixteen boys and girls at the trial, only eight would get to play in the County Cup team.

We were all really nervous, even Tabia. I went with her to see who had made the squad:

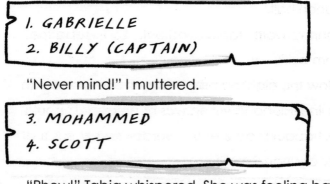

1. GABRIELLE
2. BILLY (CAPTAIN)

"Never mind!" I muttered.

3. MOHAMMED
4. SCOTT

"Phew!" Tabia whispered. She was feeling bad about tricking him like that.

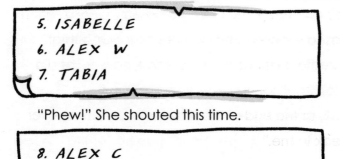

5. ISABELLE
6. ALEX W
7. TABIA

"Phew!" She shouted this time.

8. ALEX C

Surprise, surprise – my name wasn't there. Why had I even bothered going to the trial? Johnny Ball in the County Cup – who had I been kidding? What a waste of time!

"Congrats, can we go and eat now?" I asked impatiently.

My stomach was growling like there was a grizzly bear trapped inside me. I started to walk towards the lunch hall.

"Johnny, wait!" Tabia cried out. "Look, read the bottom bit!"

Below the eight names, Mr Mann had added an extra line. His handwriting was horrible, but I could still just about read the four words – four words that totally changed my life:

JOHNNY BALL – ASSISTANT MANAGER

"You can thank me later, *FISH-FART!*" Tabia grinned.

I was so shocked and confused that I asked all the questions at once. "Why, when, how, what did you do?"

"Well, at the end of the trial, Mr Mann came over to speak to me."

"What did he say?"

Tabia blew herself up like a big balloon. It was actually a really good impression of Mr Mann!

"WHAT A NUTMEG, EH? THAT'S THE SMART THINKING I'M LOOKING FOR IN MY TEAM!"

"And what did you say?"

"Actually, it was Johnny's idea."

"And what did he say?"

"JOHNNY WHO?"

Boy, this was going to take a while. "And what did you say?"

"Johnny Ball. He's a football genius."

"And what did he say?"

"OH, BALLY JUNIOR! I REMEMBER HIS BROTHER, BALLY SENIOR – A HELLUVA PLAYER HE WAS! WELL, WELL, WELL, FOOTBALL MUST RUN IN THE FAMILY…"

I could feel hope fizzing up inside of me like when you put a mint in a Coke bottle. Maybe my County Cup dream wasn't over, after all. This could be my chance to become a football genius – even if it had been an accident.

"Thanks, Tabs, you're the best best friend EVER! COUNTY CUP HERE WE COME!"

CHAPTER 5

WHAT DOES AN ASSISTANT MANAGER DO?

Johnny Ball: Assistant Manager – it sounded super cool, but what did it mean? What did an assistant manager actually do? I'm pretty sure Tissbury Primary hadn't had one for previous County Cups. EVER. What had I got myself into?

At first, I made the mistake of listening to people at school.

"Great, Johnny will be washing our dirty, stinking kits every week!" I heard Alex C shouting from the other side of the lunch hall.

Most of the time, Alex C just repeated Billy's jokes like a human-sized parrot, but sometimes he tried to make people laugh by himself. Billy didn't look that impressed, mainly because he hadn't thought of it himself. Now, he had to think of something funnier...

"Yeah, and we could do with a BALL BOY too!"

Billy yelled and, of course, everyone laughed.

Everyone except me. No way was I signing up for running around after Billy! I thought Tabia might have some better ideas, but hers were just as bad.

"Maybe the assistant manager drives the team bus?" she suggested.

"What? I can't drive a bus – I'm only nine years old!"

"Yeah, that could be a problem," she said, slowly slurping her slimy custard. "OK, maybe the assistant manager puts out the cones and hands out the water bottles. You're old enough to do that, right?"

"Yes, but that sounds SUPER BORING!"

"Well, sorr-y, *MONKEY-MOUTH!*"

No, they were all wrong, I decided. As a football player, I was good, but not that good. Now that I had accidentally become a football (assistant) manager, I was going to be great! I would use all my football genius ideas to make my family proud of me. I was going to lead Tissbury Primary to County Cup glory and become "THE NEXT PAUL PORTERFIELD"!

Paul Porterfield started out as the Tissbury Town assistant manager and now he's the manager, and probably the best manager in the whole wide world. It isn't just my dad who says that, I promise! Thanks to him, our local team has won almost as many trophies as Daniel.

In fact, I was hoping that my big brother might be able to answer my question. And it was a good chance to talk to him. When we were younger, Daniel and I used to do everything together, but now that he was in Year 9, he didn't have time to hang out with me so much. Actually, he didn't have time to hang out with me AT ALL. But if there was one thing that could get Daniel talking, it was football.

After school that day, I waited ages for my brother to get home so I could ask him all about assistant managers. When he finally arrived, he stormed straight upstairs, without even taking his earphones out.

"Nice to see you too, Daniel!" I said out loud, but only because I knew that he couldn't hear me.

I counted to 50 and then decided to be brave.

"Hello?" I called out, knocking on his bedroom door. These days, my brother has rules.

"Yeah, what's up?" he called back.

That was the sign that it was safe to enter. In the sunlight, Daniel's room sparkled like a pirate's treasure chest. There were trophies everywhere: gold, silver, bronze, big, medium, small, tournament cups, league titles, Player of the Year awards. If Daniel hadn't been a pretty good brother once upon a time, I would REALLY hate his talented football guts.

Once he'd kicked a few football magazines off the bed, there was space for me to sit down and share my news.

"Hey, I didn't make the school team..."

"That's savage – sorry, bro."

"But I'm the assistant manager instead."

"That's swipe – classy, bro."

I didn't really understand my brother's new cool-kid talk, but, of course, I pretended I did.

"Yeah, classy, bro. Anyway, WHAT DOES AN ASSISTANT MANAGER DO?"

"No clue," Daniel said, with his new cool-kid shrug. "Whatever you want, I guess."

I tried to copy Daniel's cool-kid shrug, but I think it looked more like a bad dad dance. Luckily, he ignored it and kept talking.

"Is Macho Mann still the manager? That's what we used to call him – he's so hench it's unreal, you know what I mean? The guy knows nothing about football, though – NOTHING! You know your stuff, bro, so maybs you could teach him a thing or two."

"Yeah, cool, maybs," I said as a smile spread across my face.

Suddenly, I couldn't wait to be the assistant manager – even if I didn't know what one did. I was so excited that I made a TRULY TERRIBLE MISTAKE: I told my parents.

"Assistant manager, eh?" Dad smiled. It was such big news that he even paused the football on TV. "Well done, son! Back when I was playing for the Tissbury Tigers, we didn't have an assistant manager. It was just Derek Dodds and five old footballs that were as heavy as hippos. I'm sure that's why I broke my right ankle… Did I ever tell you the story of how it happened?"

Oh no, not again! "Yes, Dad. Thanks, Dad!" I said quickly.

"Come here, my little brain-box. I'm so proud of you!" Mum screamed, hugging me so tightly that I could barely breathe. But as long as she didn't – oh no, there it was – THE DOUBLE CHEEK PINCH!

"Mum, stop! WHAT DOES AN ASSISTANT MANAGER DO?"

Apparently, she was too proud to even hear me. "We'll need to get you a smart new coat!"

"No, thanks. What does an assistant manager do?"

No answer. When Mum was in super-embarrassing mode, she was unstoppable. "You're right, a tracksuit would be better. I could even sew "JNB" on it for you. You'll look adorable!"

"No way! Please, Mum, WHAT DOES AN ASSISTANT MANAGER DO?"

"Well, you'll definitely need a clipboard," she decided.

"Mum!"

"I've got it – a pocket notebook!"

"Mum!"

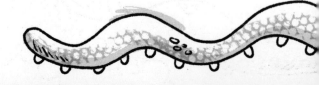

"Every top coach has a pocket notebook so they can write down their ideas."

"MUM!"

"Yes, darling?"

"WHAT.DOES.AN.ASSISTANT.MANAGER.DO?"

"Err, umm, well, they, err, umm, assist the, err, umm, manager. They help with, err, umm, you know…!"

No, I didn't know – that was the problem! There was only one person left to ask: Grandpa George. He knew lots and lots about football. When Dad wasn't around to hear her, Mum said that's who Daniel got his football skills from.

Grandpa George lives around the corner from our house, so I went over to visit him.

"What can I do for my favourite little follyflop?" Grandpa George shouted loudly, wrapping me in his really, really long arms. Imagine an octopus, but with two arms instead of eight. That's Grandpa George.

Oh, I should warn you – Grandpa George uses lots of weird, long words, which are EITHER so old that no one else remembers them, OR totally made up. I'm still not sure which.

"Assistant manager! Well, let me see … yes, yes, I was an assistant manager once upon a time, back when I was a young yabadoo. Malcolm McCleary – he was the manager and he could be a mean magubbin when he wanted to be. If the team was playing badly, he would shout himself shift-eyed!"

"What did you do, Grandpa?"

"Well, if McCleary was blowing a real blusty, I stayed out of his way!"

"No, I meant – what did you do as the assistant manager?"

"Well, I did whatever I could to help my team. I took the training sessions, I picked the players and I tried to keep everyone hippy hoppy happy. All the important thingymanoodles!"

"Did you like being an assistant manager, Grandpa?"

"Oh yes, they were the best bobby-dazzlers of my life!" he shouted so loudly that the teacups started to shake.

At last, I had an answer to my question. And

being an assistant manager sounded super fun!

Suddenly, Grandpa George's face froze in a great big grin. **_TING!_** Yes, that's where I got my light-bulb moments from. Daniel got the football skills and I got the football brains! Slowly, Grandpa George got up from his chair and went into his bedroom.

CRASH! BANG! RATTLE!

"Is everything all right, Grandpa?" I asked.

"Yes, just looking for something!"

Eventually, Grandpa George returned with a very long scarf in his hand. It had grey and orange stripes and it looked – and smelled – REALLY OLD.

"Found it!" Grandpa George said, shouting again. "My lucky scarf. When I wore this beauty, we won every malodding match!"

And with that, he handed the scarf to me. It was mine now. Wow, I didn't know what to say. Luckily, I went for, "Thanks, Grandpa!", instead of, "I think this needs a wash!"

What was I waiting for? I was now all set to become "Johnny Ball: Assistant Manager", "THE NEXT PAUL PORTERFIELD" and the future number one football genius in the whole wide world.

CHAPTER 6

THE FIRST TRAINING SESSION

When I came downstairs for breakfast on the day of my first training session, there were two things waiting for me:

1. Grandpa George's scarf, smelling clean and looking longer than ever.

2. My very own pocket notebook.

"Thanks, Mum!" I said as I munched on my cereal.

There were two problems with the notebook:

1. It had my initials on it – "JNB" – and not just on the front cover; on EVERY SINGLE PAGE!

2. It didn't fit in any of my pockets.

I didn't want to hurt Mum's feelings, so I just stuffed it in my bag, with the scarf, and set off for school.

"Go get 'em, tiger!" she shouted after me, switching to her awful American accent again.

What was I thinking? It would have been so easy to just leave the notebook and the scarf in my bag, and lie to Mum and Grandpa George. But instead, after school, I took both of them out onto the training field and gave Billy two new jokes to add to his collection.

"What is that?" he snorted, pointing at my scarf. I'd had to wrap it around my neck six times to stop it from dragging along the floor. "This is football, Harry Potter – not quidditch!"

I think you can guess what happened next – yes, everyone laughed.

"And what is that?" he cackled, pointing at the notebook in my hand. "Is that your book of spells?"

This was Billy's idea of a warm-up. I had to do something quickly before he grabbed the notebook and saw the "JNB" on the front. Remember, no one needed to know about the Nigel, especially not Billy! No, I couldn't let him complete his comedy hat-trick...

Luckily, Mr Mann chose that moment to blow his whistle, which was even louder than his booming voice.

FWEEEEEEEEEEEEEEET!

ARGHHHH, my ears! They're ringing right now just thinking about it, but at least it stopped Billy.

"RIGHT, TROOPS," Mr Mann shouted, with his huge hands on his huge hips. "WELCOME TO THE TISSBURY PRIMARY FOOTBALL TEAM! I'M NOT GOOD WITH NAMES, SO YOU'LL ALL BE GETTING NICKNAMES INSTEAD. YOU – WHAT'S YOUR NAME?"

"Scott."

"OK, FROM NOW ON, YOU'RE SCOTTY."

It wasn't hard to work out Mr Mann's "nicknames" – they all ended in a "y"! Gabrielle became "Gabby" and Mohammed became "Meddy", even

though we all call him "Mo", which is way easier
to say. Alex C and Alex W became "Clarky" and
"Webby". Our team now sounded like Snow White's
Seven Dwarfs!

"Isabelle."

"OK, FROM NOW ON, YOU'RE BELLY."

"Wait, shouldn't I be Izzy?"

"NEXT!"

"Tabia."

"OK, FROM NOW ON, YOU'RE TABBY."

"What? I'm not a cat!" Tabia muttered moodily
under her breath.

"YOU, WHAT"S YOUR NAME?"

"Billy."

Uh-oh, a name that *already* ended in a "y"! What
would Mr Mann do?

"HMMMMM, OK, FROM NOW ON, YOU'RE ... BILLY."

"But that's actually my na—"

"DONE!"

Now that all the nicknames were sorted, it seemed
like a good time for me to share my ideas with Mr
Mann, you know, assistant manager to manager.
I had spent the whole of Maths class filling pages
and pages of my pocket notebook with great ideas

for training exercises. But as soon as I started to show him…

"NOT NOW, BALLY JUNIOR – CAN'T YOU SEE I'M BUSY?" Mr Mann interrupted, swatting them away like flies. "WE'VE GOT PROPER TRAINING TO DO! RIGHT, TROOPS, LET'S START WITH THREE LAPS OF THE PITCH."

"Noooooooooooo!" everyone groaned.

"COME ON, YOU'LL NEED TO RUN YOUR SOCKS OFF IN THIS TEAM!"

What?

"DON'T LET ME DOWN! BALLY JUNIOR WILL LEAD THE WAY."

Double what? Had I heard Mr Mann right? Me? I had never run three laps in my life! I had great football ideas, not great football energy.

"BALLY JUNIOR, YOU'LL BE NEEDING ONE OF THESE," Mr Mann boomed, putting a whistle around my neck like it was an Olympic gold medal.

I still wasn't happy about him ignoring my ideas, but, wow, my very own whistle! I put it to my mouth and—

Fwe...e...t

The noise fizzled out like a rubbish firework.

Hmm, I would need to practise that. Either I was the worst whistle-blower ever, or Mr Mann had given me a cheap whistle from the pound shop. I was just the ASSISTANT manager, after all.

I threw my pocket notebook down on the grass – what a waste of time! – and covered it with Grandpa George's super-long scarf. I started jogging. For the first 100 metres, I felt powerful. I was the team leader and I had the whistle to prove it.

But then I got a stitch.

"What's wrong?" Tabia asked me. She wasn't even sweating yet.

"N-noth-ing," I panted.

By the corner flag, we stopped to do some stretching. Well, that's what I told everyone, but really, I just needed a rest. Boy, running is super tiring! On the third lap, I felt like I was going to collapse, but somehow I made it to the finish line.

"THANKS, BALLY JUNIOR," Mr Mann said, putting away his phone. "RIGHT, TROOPS, I SUPPOSE WE SHOULD PRACTISE A BIT OF PASSING AND SHOOTING. WHAT ARE YOU WAITING FOR? LET'S GO, LET'S GO!"

Passing and shooting! It wasn't exactly rocket science, but at least it was better than just playing a match.

Luckily, Billy was in Mr Mann's group, but I did have a miserable-looking Alex C to deal with. The parrot was missing his master.

"What are you looking at, SPITBALL?" he huffed in my direction.

Not bad! I hadn't heard that one before, so I guess he must have come up with it himself. I didn't reply, though. Instead, I clapped my hands together to signal the start of my amazing coaching career.

"Right, troops," I said, putting on my best mini-Mr-Mann performance (only without the silly football people language). "Is everyone ready? I want you to play the pass and then keep running forward for the one-two. Tabs, show them how it's done!"

She passed the ball to me and I passed it back (see, I told you I can kick the ball!). Then, Tabia shot it top right bins.

"Perfect!" I cheered.

PASS, PASS, SHOT!

Bottom left bins – "Nice one, Scott!"

PASS, PASS, SHOT!

Post and in – "Yes, Iz!"

PASS, PASS, SHOT!

Alex C blazed the ball high over the bar.

"Unlucky. Take your time with your next shot! Aim for one of the corners…"

What was I thinking? Trying to give advice to Tabia or Scott was fine, but to Billy's sidekick? No chance! As the words slipped out of my mouth, I tried to shove them back in, but it was too late.

"…if you want," I added.

Alex C glared back at me. "What do YOU know? If your pass wasn't so pants, I would have scored easily!"

I stayed silent, but, like always, my best friend had my back.

"Don't be such a **DONKEY-DOUGHNUT** – you missed by a mile!" Tabia shouted. "Johnny's our assistant manager now and he's just trying to help. Trust me, he's a football genius!"

Alex C didn't say sorry, but he didn't say anything else mean either. His next shot was way, way better. He took his time, he stayed calm and he scored.

You're welcome! I thought to myself, but this time, I managed to keep my big mouth shut.

Mr Mann soon got bored and brought both groups together for, yep, you guessed it – a match.

"BALLY JUNIOR, YOU'RE IN CHARGE!" he boomed, getting out his phone.

GULP! Me? Sure, I know every football rule there's ever been, but with Billy watching me, would I even be able to get my whistle to work?

"Come on, Johnny, LET'S PLAY BALL!" he joked as I fumbled around with it.

Of course, everyone laughed, but not as loudly as usual. Maybe the team didn't mind their new assistant manager, after all…

Anyway, hopefully you'll be pleased to hear that Johnny Ball: Referee didn't do too badly:

I didn't give any silly penalties,

I didn't trip over my own feet,

I didn't get a stitch,

and, best of all, I didn't get hit by another one of Billy's big HOOFs!

WIN, WIN, WIN, MEGA WIN!

Unfortunately, the Tissbury Primary players weren't doing quite so well.

Billy's HOOFs! kept flying way over Tabia's head. There were no MAD SKILLZ to be seen; only MAD PLAYERZ.

"What was that, *NUGGET-NOSE?*"

"As if you could do any better, *TABBY-CAT!*"

Mo couldn't pass the ball forward,

Izzy couldn't pass at all,

Scott couldn't stop slide-tackling,

Alex W couldn't start scoring,

and Gabby? Well, she didn't have anything to do in goal!

No, it wasn't looking good for the team, but at least I had got through the first training session. Phew! Soon, it would be time for the first match. Would it be a dream debut for Johnny Ball: Assistant Manager, or the early end of my career as an accidental football genius?

CHAPTER 7

"SICKY" SAVES THE DAY!

TISSBURY PRIMARY VS LAMBERT PRIMARY

"Lambert? Man, they're TOTES TRAGIC!" Daniel told me at breakfast, showing off some more of his new cool-kid talk. "We beat them, like, 12–1, and Macho Mann took me off after, like, 10 minutes. He said it was 'the sporting thing to do', or something stank like that. You'll thrash them, bro, no probs!"

Really? My brother hadn't seen our team play yet. It wasn't pretty! Put it this way – we looked a lot more like Bristol Rovers than Brazil. Daniel had made me feel a tiny bit better about our chances, but my tummy still felt like a busy butterfly jail.

Why was I so nervous? It wasn't like I had to PLAY in the match! No, I was just the assistant manager – all I had to do was watch and, hopefully, help…

But I couldn't even enjoy my favourite meal ever – Mum's "Three-a-Fried" breakfast.

YUMMY! She didn't even need to ask me what was wrong. Mums already know everything, don't they?

"Don't worry, you'll be great, and I'll be there to chee—"

"What?" I nearly spat a mouthful of super-tasty sausage across the table.

"I said I'll be there to cheer you on. I wouldn't miss my baby's first match as assistant manager!"

"Mum, no!"

No, no, no – I couldn't have my MUM there. That would be SUPER EMBARRASSING! She would definitely say something, probably in her awful American accent. How could I stop her? I looked at Daniel, but he just gave a cool-kid shrug.

"OK, fine, but NO CHEERING!"

"Me? Cheer? Of course not, dearest. You won't even know I'm there..."

♔ ♔ ♔

"ATTA BOY, JOHNNYKINS!" Mum was cheering and clapping before the game had even kicked off. She wasn't the only parent there, but she was the only one making way too much noise.

So, I did what I always do when my mum is SUPER EMBARRASSING – I hid behind my hand and focused on football.

"Johnny, how was Tissbury's first match?" you ask. Well, if my teacher, Miss Patel, asked me to write a poem about it, I would describe it as:

> Slipping and Sliding.
> Hoofing and hiding.
> owwing and offsiding!

Basically, it was the second-worst game of football I've ever seen:

1. Tissbury Town vs Wopham Wanderers in the pouring rain: 0–0.

2. Tissbury Primary vs Lambert Primary.

As soon as the match kicked off, the players swarmed around the ball like flies around a dog poo.

KICK! Then CHASE!
KICK! Then CHASE!

It was awful! Whatever they were playing, it definitely wasn't football.

Was Mr Mann tearing his invisible hair out on the touchline? Oh no, he was too busy on his phone, checking to see how his beloved Blether United were doing.

Then, out of the blue, our striker, Alex W, had an awesome chance to score. He was two yards out, with an open goal in front of him ... but somehow, he scooped the ball over the bar! Noooooooo! It was like Alex W's foot had suddenly turned into a spade.

It was even worse than Alex C's miss in training. I, the boy some *GECKO-GUTS* call Johnny "Can't

Kick The" Ball, would definitely have scored, but let's not get into that...

"How did you miss THAT?" Billy yelled at Alex W, instead of me for once. "It was an absolute sitter!"

Poor Alex W hadn't exactly been Mr Confident to start with, but after that bad miss and then Billy's mean words, he was too scared to even go near the ball.

The half-time score was Tissbury Primary 0, Lambert Primary 0. Sadly, the football didn't get any better in the second half either.

"THAT'S IT – SMASH IT!" Mr Mann boomed as Billy achieved his highest HOOF! yet.

No, PASS it! I said over and over again in my head, just in case Tabs could read my thoughts. *Spread out – there's so much space to play PROPER football!*

I could hardly bear to watch. It was like the time in Year 4 when Mr Tufnell taught us about electrical circuits. He gave us lots of wires and showed us how to connect them up to make the little light bulb shine. But when we tried ourselves, Tabia and I kept getting it wrong. Those wiggly wires were all over our desk, in all the wrong places.

And that's exactly how our team looked now; the players were all over the pitch, in all the wrong places. It was as if Mr Mann hadn't even given them positions, but he had!

Scott was meant to be a defender, but instead, he was chasing up the pitch after every "pass".

Tabs was meant to be our attacking playmaker, but instead, she had dropped deeper and deeper to try and get on the ball.

And Billy was meant to be bossing the midfield, but instead, he was just bellowing at the other players, while walking around like it was still the warm-up!

I knew exactly what Dad would say about Billy: "Lots of huff and puff, but he won't be blowing any houses down!" I'd heard Dad say that about lots of Tissbury Town players at Railway Road Stadium. He could be pretty funny sometimes when he wasn't boasting about Daniel or moaning about his right ankle.

Somehow, with five minutes to go, it was still Tissbury 0, Lambert 0. What could I do to get my team to shine more brightly? We had to score – and quickly.

"SUBS, ARE YOU READY?" That was Mr Mann's masterplan.

"Yes, Coach!" said "Clarky".

"Yes, Coach!" said "Belly".

"Y-yes, C-coach," mumbled "Meddy" from behind his hand.

SNIFF, SNIFF – UGHHHHH!

What was that HORRIBLE, AWFUL, STINKING SMELL? And where was it coming from?

It didn't take me long to work it out. Mo's face gave it away – it was almost as green as the grass.

"Are you feeling OK, mate?" I asked, covering my nose and mouth with Grandpa George's scarf. Finally, I had a use for it and it was so long that it could have protected Mr Mann too!

"Yes, better now," Mo said, wiping PUKE from his face. It was all over his shirt too.

UGHHHHH!

Was he ill or just nervous? It didn't matter, because ***TING! LIGHT-BULB MOMENT!*** At last! I had been waiting all game for one and now it had arrived, just in time. I ran straight over to Mr Mann.

"I've got an idea!" I said and then whispered it to him.

Mr Mann frowned and then looked over at Mo. He was now wiping his pukey mouth with his pukey shirt.

UGHHHHH!

"YOU SURE ABOUT THIS, BALLY JUNIOR?" he boom-whispered back.

I nodded eagerly.

"OK, WELL, WE'VE GOT NOTHING TO LOSE!" he admitted. "MEDDY, GO OUT THERE AND GET UP FRONT."

"B-but I'm a d-defender," he moaned.

What could we do? We didn't want to shout it out and spoil the plan, but we also didn't want to get close enough to Mo to whisper.

TING! SMALLER LIGHT-BULB MOMENT! I wrote the plan down in the pocket notebook Mum had given me, ripped the page out and made it into a paper aeroplane.

Mo read it and then stumbled onto the field and straight into the Lambert penalty area.

SNIFF, SNIFF – UGHHHHH!

What was that HORRIBLE, AWFUL, STINKING SMELL? And where was it coming from?

The Lambert players soon worked it out – they could see the puke all over Mo's shirt.

"No way, I'm not marking him!" one said, holding his nose.

"Neither am I!"

"Neither am I!"

"Neither am I!"

When Billy eventually got the ball off Izzy after her tenth dribble in a circle, he HOOFed! it forward. Mo was standing there all by his pukey self, in loads of pukey space. He pulled back his shaking leg and **BANG!** It wasn't a great shot, but the Lambert goalkeeper slipped (or maybe he fainted because of that HORRIBLE, AWFUL, STINKING SMELL)…

Either way, the ball rolled slowly over the goal-line. 1–0 to Tissbury!

GOOOOOOOOAAAAAAAALLLL!

"MO, YOU HERO!" The team were shouting, but as they ran towards him, they stopped. UGHHHHH! It was like they hit a solid wall of HORRIBLE, AWFUL, STINKING SMELL.

"NICE ONE, I'LL CALL YOU 'SICKY' FROM NOW ON!" Mr Mann boomed like it was the best joke ever.

"Get in. We're gonna win the County Cup!" Billy cheered.

What planet was he on? If it hadn't been for my great football idea, we wouldn't even have won our first game – against LAMBERT PRIMARY! No, we had a long, long, long way to go. Longer even than Grandpa George's scarf.

"Congratulations, Johnny-bun!" Mum squealed from the sidelines. "What happened at the end there? Bless him, Mohammed did very well, but why wasn't anyone marking him? And surely that keeper could have done a little bit better…"

"No idea," I said, smiling to myself.

MATCH REPORT 1   ✍ JNB

TISSBURY PRIMARY 1–0 LAMBERT PRIMARY

STARTING LINE-UP (MARKS OUT OF 10):
Gabby 5, Scotty 5, Billy 3, Tabby 6, Webby 4

SUBS:
Belly 5, Clarky 5, Meddy/"Sicky" 10!

SCORER:
Meddy/"Sicky"

C+

WHAT WENT WELL:
We won (thanks to me!)

EVEN BETTER IF:
List too long!

CHAPTER 8

THE LEGEND OF LENNY LOMAS

As soon as we got home after the Lambert match, I went straight over to Grandpa George's house to tell him the super-great news. I left out the part about using his scarf as a stink mask, obviously.

"Ho, ho, HO!" he laughed loudly. "What a TIDDLYTASTIC trick!"

"I'm glad we didn't lose in the first round," I said with a sigh, "but I think that's it for us. Our team is terrible!"

OK, to prove it, I'm going to show you something top, top secret right now, but you've got to promise me you won't share this with ANYONE, OK? Good, because if any of the Tissbury Primary players read this, I'll be in super-big trouble!

PLAYER NOTES

GABBY
Zero shots, zero saves, no problems ... yet

SCOTTY
Loves ice cream and tackling, doesn't love staying back

BILLY
Lots of HOOFing! not much moving

TABBY
Thank goodness we've got her!

WEBBY
Puts the "er" in "striker", NOT the next
Johnny Jeffries

SUBS:

BELLY
Silky skills, but never passes

CLARKY
~~Hammer head, but is he right-footed or~~
~~left-footed? Still not sure!~~

MEDDY/"SICKY"
Decent, but needs to work on fitness

So now you see what I mean, right? The Tissbury
Primary team was totally terrible!

But Grandpa George didn't see it that way.
"Hmmm, well you've got wallops of work to do
then, my boy!"

"Me? It's not MY fault that our striker can't even
score with an open goal!"

"No, but you can help him to hit the hooting
net, can't you? You're the assistant manager,
miladdy! Football is all about working together,
and confidence goes a luverly long way. Have I

ever told you about little Lenny Lomas? No? Oh, this is a stupendous story! Lenny was our teeny-weeny star striker for years and everyone loved him. The manager, Malcolm McCleary, loved him more than his own wife and children put together! But one day, Lenny just stopped scoring, all in a jiffy. His confidence had gone up the chuffing chimney. It was like he had never seen a football in his lemonading life! Old McCleary tried everything:

giving him a hard time,

giving him a hug,

buying him new boots,

buying him new teammates

– but NOTHING worked. It was a muddy mystery! Eventually, old McCleary turned to me and he said, 'Jaws!' – that was my nickname back then, don't ask me why – 'HELP ME!'

"In training, Lenny was as barfstorming as ever – he could score from anywhere! It was only in matches that he froze like snot in the snow. *TING!* I had a mahoosive *LIGHT-BULB MOMENT!* I knew that little Lenny worked for an animal charity, so I told him: 'The next time you're about to shoot, imagine that the goal is one of those hopping horrible hunters.

You want to hit that hunter really hard but the goalkeeper – he's the luverly lion that you're trying to save. Whatever you do, DON'T HIT HIM!'"

"And did the plan work, Grandpa?" I asked impatiently. I needed to know how the story ended.

"It worked a tricker treat! When the chance arrived, Lenny looked up and leathered the ball straight into the top corner. 'Take that, Herbert!' he roared."

"Who's Herbert?"

Grandpa George shrugged. "The hopping horrible hunter, I guess. Anyway, old McCleary jumped on me and gave me a hug for the first and only time. 'Jaws, you beauty!' he yellered. 'How did you do it?'

"When I told him, he gave a mahoosive lot of money to Save the Lions!"

"And after that, Grandpa? Did he keep scoring?"

"Oh yes, that was the end of the Lenny Lomas Goal Drought of 1952!"

TING! LIGHT-BULB MOMENT! for me. I was going to help turn Alex W into the next Lenny Lomas … no, the next Johnny "The Rocket" Jeffries!

"Thanks, Grandpa!" I said, rushing out the door.

"My word, where are you off to in such a rabbity rush?"

"Sorry, Grandpa, I can't stay. I've got wallops of work to do!"

🏆 🏆 🏆

Unfortunately, Alex W didn't really like lions.

"I prefer tigers," he told me when I asked him at training. He didn't even seem surprised by the question. Maybe people asked him that a lot. "Mammals aren't really my thing, though."

"Interesting," I replied, doing my best serious journalist impression. I even moved my hand towards his mouth like it was a microphone. "So, what is your thing?"

"*Kyoto Dragons*, this new Japanese anime show."

I hadn't even heard of it, but, of course, I nodded along like I had. It was clear that Alex W really, really loved it – way more than he loved scoring goals, that's for sure. If it hadn't been for Mr Mann's whopping great whistle, he would have kept talking about it for hours.

"All of the characters are just so awesome! My favourite is Koyo. What about you?"

"Yeah, er, that's my favourite too," I agreed. Was Koyo a human or a dragon? Was it a he or a she? There was only one way to find out.

When I got home, the TV was there waiting for me. Yes! I sunk happily into the sofa. Dad and Daniel were out at Tissbury Tigers training, and Mum? She was somewhere upstairs, so if I turned the volume right down, I—

"Johnny Nigel Ball!" a voice called out.

Uh-oh – not my full name! There was Mum, walking down the stairs, doing her "I'm very disappointed in you" face.

"Come on, you know the rules," she said firmly.

"No TV until you've finished your homework."

"This IS my homework!" I argued. "My assistant manager homework!"

I explained everything – Alex W, Grandpa George, Lenny Lomas, *Kyoto Dragons* – and eventually Mum held up both her hands and did her "I've heard enough!" face.

"You've got ten minutes, OK? Then you've got to do your real homework. I'm timing you!"

It's a good thing that I'm super fast with the TV

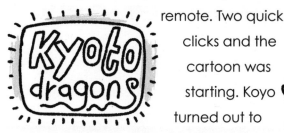

remote. Two quick clicks and the cartoon was starting. Koyo turned out to

be a young boy with big, spiky hair who looked after five different-coloured dragons and sent them out on special rescue missions. It was actually a pretty cool show.

"Right, time's up, poppet!" Mum yelled from the kitchen.

Already? But I didn't yet know if Rinko (the red one) had saved Kyoto City from the professor's evil plan!

"If you get all your homework done, you can watch the rest before bed, OK?" Mum promised.

DEAL! I raced through my Maths homework at record speed. I mostly hate Maths, but it turns out short division can be quite fun when there's a TV show waiting at the end.

"Finished!" I called out, like it was one of Miss Patel's tricky spelling tests.

(Spoiler alert: Rinko did save Kyoto City. Go, Rinko!) By the time the episode was over, I had what I needed: a super-clever plan to solve my own Lenny Lomas problem.

CHAPTER 9

KOYO KICKS THE FLAME-ROCK!

TISSBURY PRIMARY VS SHEPHERD'S CROSS PRIMARY

"Shepherd's Cross? They're, like, literally DAMP!"
Daniel told me as we travelled to Tissbury Primary's
second match. Don't worry, my big brother wasn't
coming to watch – no way! No, we both had
games at the same time on the same day, and
there was only one car to drive us around: Tiss.

Tiss is named after Tiss the Tiger, the Tissbury Town
mascot. He's orange on the outside and football on
the inside:

black and white seats,

black and white steering wheel

and a black and white bumper sticker that says
FOOTBALL FAMILY ON BOARD (just in case people
hadn't worked that out already!).

Anyway, back to Daniel's cool-kid description.
"Damp" – did that mean Shepherd's Cross were

good or bad? It sounded bad, but it was hard to know.

"We didn't even have to play them because they always got knocked out in the first round," my brother explained. "But maybe they've got better."

I really hoped they hadn't. Tissbury had needed a puking player just to beat Lambert. How could we possibly win the second round?

"No, we can do this," I told myself calmly as we pulled into the car park. We had to believe in ourselves, and I had to help my team.

"Let's go, champ!" Mum called out a little too loudly as she opened the door for me.

🏆 🏆 🏆

"Wait!" I called out when I saw Alex W walking onto the school field to warm up for the match. By the time I reached him, I was totally out of breath.

"Koyo," I gasped and he smiled straight away. It was like the secret password to unlock his bonus happy level.

"Have you seen the latest episode yet?" Alex W asked.

This time, I didn't have to pretend. "The one

where Rinko saved Kyoto City from the professor's evil plan? Yeah, it was super exciting!"

Alex W and I were BFFs now. Part one of my plan was complete, so it was time for part two. It was time for me to be Johnny Ball: Assistant Manager.

"You know the part where Koyo had to get the flame-rocks past the evil professor and into the dragons' den?" I said.

"Yeah?"

"Well, when you get the chance to shoot today, imagine that the goal is the dragons' den and the ball is a flame-rock."

He looked confused, so I carried on.

"The dragons need that flame-rock in order to rescue Princess Juyo, but the goalkeeper is the evil professor who's trying to stop you. Whatever you do, YOU HAVE TO GET IT PAST HIM!"

At first, Alex W was silent, but I could tell that he was thinking about it because he was looking up as if he was trying to see into his own brain.

"Cool, thanks, it's worth a try!" he said eventually.

"GO, JOHNNY-BOO!" Mum cheered as the match kicked off. Yes, she was back and just as super embarrassing as ever. But when I put up my hand-shield, she totally disappeared. Perfect, now I could focus on the football...

I wouldn't call it a good first half, but it was a bit better than the last one. For a start, there was ONE whole goal! Tabs showed off her MAD SKILLZ to make it 1–0 to Tissbury.

"THAT'S MY GIRL!" I could hear my mum shouting, even through my hand-shield.

Blether United weren't playing, so Mr Mann was watching properly this time. "WHAT A SCREAMER!" he boomed.

"Yes, Tabs!" I muttered to myself, punching the air. Again, we would save our special, secret handshake for later.

Maybe we wouldn't need one of my football ideas after all...

Oh yes, we would! Mr Mann had picked "Sicky" in the starting line-up after his winner against Lambert, but he looked super nervous about all that extra game time. We took him off just before he puked all over the pitch.

"BELLY, ON YOU GO AND GET STUCK IN!"

Izzy did get involved straight away, but not in the way that Mr Mann had hoped. As the ball came to her, she was in single-player mode again, just like against Lambert. It was as if she was playing football in her own really dark, loud tunnel and couldn't see her teammates all around her, or hear them calling out: "PASS! PASS!"

Instead, Izzy kept her head down and the ball stuck to her foot, but she wasn't dribbling through the defence to score a wonder goal. No, she was going around and around in circles! Eventually, she got so dizzy that she fell over and Shepherd's Cross ran through and equalized.

"I was right THERE!" Billy bellowed at her. He hadn't even bothered to try and chase back. "Why don't you ever PASS?"

As always, Tabia had her friend's back. "Hey, leave her alone, **BABOON-BUM!** Why don't you try doing something useful for a change?"

By half-time, Alex W had only touched the ball twice. The first time, a HOOF! from Billy hit him in the back of the head and the second time, a goal kick from Gabby bobbled off his boot. There had been zero shots … so far.

"Come on, Koyo!" I whispered to him as the players walked on for the second half, hoping that the secret password would work again. "Don't forget the flame-rock!"

As he went back out onto the pitch, Alex W walked a bit taller. He hadn't exactly been small to start with, but now he was a giant! When the second half kicked off, he chased around the pitch like a giraffe in a jam jar.

"WHOA, WHAT'S GOT INTO WEBBY?" Mr Mann boom-asked me.

"No idea," I said, smiling to myself.

Alex W just needed a chance now. When Tabia

came over to take a throw-in, I gave her the game plan.

"Really? I've never seen him kick the ball properly, let alone score!"

"Trust me."

"OK, OK!"

A few minutes later, Tabia skilled her way down the left wing again and crossed to Alex W just inside the Shepherd's Cross penalty area. This was it! I couldn't bear to watch, but at the same time, I couldn't stop watching.

First touch – fine. The ball was under control.

I tried my best to tunnel into his mind: "Get the flame-rock past the evil professor, get the flame-rock past the evil professor..."

Second touch - **WHACK!**

KOYOOOOOOO!

"GOOOOOOOOAAAAAAALLLL!"

shouted Mr Mann.

2–1 to Tissbury!

I could see the ball in the back of the net, but at first, I didn't believe my eyes. Neither did Alex W. What had just happened? We both just stood there in shock as everyone else went wild. Thanks, Grandpa George, thanks, little Lenny Lomas!

"You did it, Webby!" a much-recovered Mo shouted, jumping up on Alex W's back.

"Nice finish!" Billy said. "I would have scored it, obviously, but I didn't think *you* would."

Scott came on and helped the defence stay strong for the last few minutes until the final whistle. Yes, we were through to the third round!

And it was all thanks to Alex W (and Tabia, of course, but she's always the star). All the players hugged and high-fived him. He was a hero now! Eventually, he managed to fight his way out of Billy's big team bundle and find me.

"Thanks, Johnny!" Alex W cried out, lifting me into the air. "Mr Mann, our Koyo plan worked perfectly – Johnny's a football genius!"

"No, it was all your work – what a strike!" I replied

modestly; but he was right, of course. It was my new greatest football idea EVER.

So far so good for Johnny Ball: Assistant Manager. Mr Mann gave me a massive pat on the back that nearly sent me flying.

"TOP JOB, BALLY JUNIOR. LET'S KEEP UP THE WINNING WORK!"

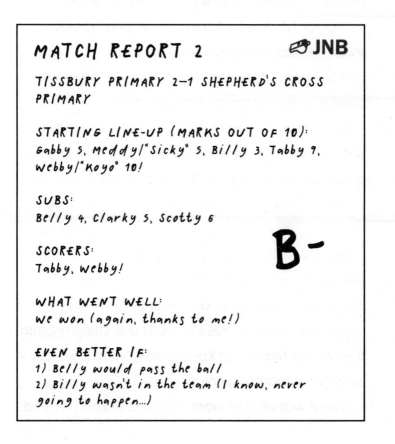

MATCH REPORT 2　　　🖊**JNB**

TISSBURY PRIMARY 2—1 SHEPHERD'S CROSS PRIMARY

STARTING LINE-UP (MARKS OUT OF 10):
Gabby 5, Meddy/"Sicky" 5, Billy 3, Tabby 9, Webby/"Koyo" 10!

SUBS:
Belly 4, Clarky 5, Scotty 6

SCORERS:
Tabby, Webby!

B-

WHAT WENT WELL:
We won (again, thanks to me!)

EVEN BETTER IF:
1) Belly would pass the ball
2) Billy wasn't in the team (I know, never going to happen...)

CHAPTER 10

NO ONE LIKES A BALL GROG!

We were all really excited after the Shepherd's Cross game. Well, all of us except "Dizzy Izzy". She was still feeling bad about not passing.

"Don't sweat it, sister!" Mum told Izzy in her awful American accent.

She'd hoped it might help, but it didn't. Izzy didn't even smile. That's because Mum isn't as funny as she thinks she is; she's mainly just SUPER EMBARRASSING.

"Mr Mann's going to drop me from the team," Izzy muttered miserably.

"No, he won't," I said, as if Mr Mann actually listened to me. "Don't worry!"

I was the assistant manager and that meant it was my job to assist. I had to find a way to help Izzy, just like I'd helped Alex W. But how? What could I do to make her pass the ball? Could the Lenny Lomas plan work again?

What if I told her the ball was a piping-hot potato that would burn her boot if she kept it for too long?

Or what if I told her the ball was a pet guinea pig that would die if it stopped rolling?

DON'T LET ME STOP!

No, if I told Izzy that, she wouldn't kick the ball at all! What I needed was a brand-new football idea.

The next day, I wandered around school, waiting for one of my light-bulb moments, but that just wasn't working.

I wore my assistant manager's scarf – nothing!

I opened my assistant manager's notebook at a fresh page – nothing!

I read the latest issue of *Kickaround* magazine from cover to cover – nothing!

My brain was as empty as Mr Flake's ice-cream van on a hot summer's day.

I thought about asking Daniel for help, but I knew he would be too busy. He had cool-kid stuff to do, like scoring goals and shrugging. So instead, I decided to go and see Grandpa George again.

"Well, if it isn't my clever little collybobble! How'd you get on?"

This time, I gave Grandpa George my full match report – Tabia's "screamer", Alex W's winner and Izzy's error.

"Oh, deary diddums," he said, "no one likes a ball grog!"

"A what?"

"A ball grog! That's what we used to call someone who thinks they can dribble around the whole tiddly team on their own."

"Do you mean a ball HOG, Grandpa?"

"Hmm, well, let me see … no, no, it was absatootly a ball GROG! Anyway, football is a team game. Perhaps, you need to remind this Izzy about that."

"Yes, but how do I do that, Grandpa?"

"Well now, you're the assistant manager, miladdy, not me!"

Grandpa George was right; it was my job to come up with another super-clever plan. What could help the Tissbury players to work together as a team? A tug of war? A relay race? No, what I needed to find out was Izzy's *Kyoto Dragons* – what was her favourite thing in the whole wide world? Once I knew that, I could use it to show her that working together was the best way to win.

🏆 🏆 🏆

"Me, of course – I'm her favourite thing!" was Tabia's first answer, when I asked her the next day.

"Very funny. Come on, this is serious."

"OK, let me think … a-ha, I've got it. Donna Does Dance!"

"Who's Donna? I didn't know Izzy had a sister."

"No, she's a famous dancer from America, *HIPPO-HEAD*. She does these really cool videos with her friends, Michael and Michelle. Where have you been for the last few weeks? You should really check it out."

"Thanks, Tabs, I will!"

The only problem was that apparently, I was still too young to have my own phone. I would have to watch it on TV, but I knew what Mum would say:

"No TV until you've finished your homework."

Unless! Unless, I told a little white lie…

"Mum, we've been learning this dance in class and we've got to perform it in assembly tomorrow," I told her as calmly as I could. "I'm really bad at it, so can I watch the video tonight please?"

"Of course," she said. But I wasn't getting away with it that easily. "Why don't I help you? We can practise together! You know, your mama used to be a real mover and groover back in her day! What kind of dance is it? Salsa? Tango? Ballet?"

"Er, it's easier if I just show you, I think."

I picked the video right at the top of the search page, called "HIPZ & HOPZ". It turned out to be a lot of hip wiggling, and a lot of hopping.

"THIS IS FUN!" Mum shouted over the loud music. "Come on, left foot forward, then SHAKE, then HOP and ... right foot forward. That's it!"

Before I knew it, I was dancing with my mum! I was so glad that the living room curtains were closed. Imagine if Billy had seen me.

Johnny BALLROOM DANCER!

Johnny DISCO BALL!

The jokes would have lasted for ever. The things I do for my football team...

Mum was having the time of her life and, if I'm 120 per cent honest, I was having a pretty good time too, once I got the hang of it.

Left foot forward, then SHAKE, then HOP and ... right foot forward...

When Dad and Daniel got home from football training, they couldn't believe their eyes.

"Come and join in, you two!" Mum called out.

"Not a chance, fam," Daniel mumbled as he raced upstairs to his room.

"Sure, why not?" Dad said, joining in, but he was totally HOPELESS! You know how they say that bad dancers have "two left feet"? Well, it was like Dad had two lazy fly swats instead.

After getting the moves wrong for the millionth time, Dad suddenly started limping.

"Let me guess, your right ankle?" Mum asked, rolling her eyes in a triple loop the loop.

Boy, what a workout! As we waved goodbye to Donna on the TV screen, I was sweating like crazy. But at least I knew what my new great football idea would be.

🏆 🏆 🏆

The next day at school, I went to see Mr Mann in his office at breaktime. Unfortunately, I was going to need his help.

"A DANCE-OFF?" he said. He sounded really surprised, as if I'd just told him that I'd been called up to play for England.

"I know it sounds strange, Sir, but it'll work, I promise. A dance competition is the perfect way to show Izzy – I mean "Belly" – the importance of teamwork. If we put her in a group with Alex C – I mean "Clarky" – and Billy, then she won't be able to win on her own. They'll have no choice but to work TOGETHER!"

Mr Mann definitely wasn't sure about my dance-off idea, but he was sure that he wanted me out of his office so that he could watch some more Blether United highlights on his phone.

"FINE, YOU CAN HAVE THE FIRST TWENTY MINUTES OF TRAINING, BALLY JUNIOR. BUT AFTER THAT, WE NEED TO PRACTISE FOOTBALL!"

🏆 🏆 🏆

FWEEEEEEEEET!

Arghhhh – our ears!

"RIGHT, TROOPS, FIRST THINGS FIRST – WELL DONE FOR BEATING SHEPHERD'S CROSS!" Mr Mann boomed and all the Tissbury players cheered loudly.

"NOW, BEFORE WE PLAY SOME ACTUAL FOOTBALL, WE'RE GOING TO DO A ER ... FUN ER ... TEAM-BUILDING EXERCISE. ISN'T THAT RIGHT, BALLY JUNIOR?"

"Boooooooooo!"

I could hear the groans already, and I hadn't even told them what the "fun team-building exercise" was yet. What if it had been a water-pistol war at the beach, or an inflatable unicorn race at Tissbury Rapids?

Uh-oh, was this going to be my first terrible football idea? There was only one way to find out. I put my whistle to my mouth and—

Fwe...e...t

Oh dear, not a good start.

"R-right, troops," I carried on with my best mini-Mr-Mann performance again. "Your challenge today is to come up with the best dance routine for this song. Don't let me down!"

HIT IT! I pressed play and the drumbeat boomed out of the assembly hall speakers. I had spent ages trying to find a half-decent song in my dad's "damp" CD collection. What song would Donna dance to? In the end, I went for "Mr Funk Skunk" by Frankie Panky and the Loverats.

He doesn't smell so good,
But he dances like a dude,
MR FUNK SKUNK!

While the song played, I watched the faces in front of me. Was it going down well?

Billy stood there with his arms folded, looking as moody as a bull in a bookshop.

Alex C, of course, just copied exactly what Billy did. But I could see Gabby, Alex W and Scott nodding their heads and tapping their feet. They were smiling, which was a good sign, although it was pretty hard not to smile at "Mr Funk Skunk"!

Mo, Tabia and Izzy, meanwhile, were loving it. They were already "throwing shapes", as my dad likes to call it.

"So Group A will be Tabby, Meddy, Webby and Gabby..." I explained, once the song had ended. "And Group B will be Belly, Billy, Clarky and Scotty."

"Belly" did not look happy at all, and neither did the rest of her group.

"Oi, DISCO BALL, what's this got to do with FOOTBALL?" Billy bellowed. "Besides, dancing's for GIRLS!"

"No, it's not! It's all about working together," I replied, "as a TEAM."

My voice was shaking a little, but I had to stay strong. I was the assistant manager, after all. "Mr Mann and I will be looking for great dance moves, but also great teamwork. Your ten minutes start ... NOW!"

Izzy burst into action. "OK, guys, let's start with the main part. So when Frankie Panky sings "MR FUNK SKUNK", we'll all pinch our noses and shake our way down to the floor like this. Yes?"

"No! Who put you in charge, Bossy Boots?" Billy asked, with his arms still folded. "I'm the Tissbury captain, not you!"

"I was just trying to help! Johnny said we had to work together and—"

"Oh, so now you want to work together, do you?" Billy interrupted. "It didn't look that way against Shepherd's Cross!"

"I'm sorry, I should have passed more. It won't happen again, OK? Come on, we've only got a few minutes left to plan our routine! Teammates?"

Izzy offered her hand. Would they, or wouldn't they? It was like one of those silly rom-coms that Mum and Dad like to watch (even though Dad pretends to hate them). Eventually, Billy shook Izzy's hand. "Teammates."

FWEEEEEEEEET!

Arghhhh – our ears!

"RIGHT, TROOPS, TIME'S UP! GROUP A, LET'S SEE WHAT YOU'VE GOT," Mr Mann boomed, while looking really bored. Maybe I should have made him join in with the dancing!

Anyway, Group A were awesome. They moved

and grooved like a real team, pulling all kinds of super-great shapes:

THAT SMELLS BAD HAND WAVE

OCTOPUS ARMS

THE TAIL SHAKE

"Excellent!" I cheered. "OK, over to you, Group B!"

Was it going to be a total disaster? As they walked to the front, Izzy and Billy were whispering to each other. Was it a team talk, or a nasty name battle? I couldn't tell.

"MR FUNK SKUNK" started to play and the group...

Wow, the group were all moving to the music ... TOGETHER!

The Wobbly Jelly,

the Steering Wheel,

and the "That Smells Bad!" Nose Pinch!

I was super impressed, and there was still time for a grand finale. Izzy looked over at Billy and nodded. Izzy leant back and kicked out her leg like she was out on the football pitch. Billy caught her foot and then kicked out his leg towards Scott. Scott caught it and kicked out his leg towards Alex C, who leant back and threw out his leg and his arm at the same time. Together, they formed a shape like a zigzag...

"LIGHTNING BOLT!" they called out together.

"Whoooooooop!" I cheered. "We have our winners. Congratulations, Group B!"

Izzy and Billy high-fived happily like actual teammates. My plan had worked!

When I got home after school, Mum was waiting for me at the front door.

"So...?" she asked.

"So, what?"

"The dance, darling dearest! How did it go?"

Oh yeah, I had completely forgotten about my little white lie.

"Thanks, Mum," I said with a big grin on my face. "Actually, it went even better than I'd expected!"

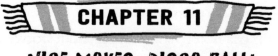

CHAPTER 11

NICE MOVES, DISCO BALL!

TISSBURY PRIMARY VS BARTLEY MOOR PRIMARY

I didn't even have to ask Daniel about Bartley
Moor; I already knew that they were a really, really
good team. They had won their first two matches
12–0 and 8–1. And to make matters worse, Mr Mann
had picked a super-attacking line-up, with ZERO
DEFENDERS! If we weren't careful, Bartley would
squash us as flat as a pancake.

The Tissbury players just had to work together
and hope for the best. I mean, what else could we
do? Well, that's what I was thinking about as Mum
and Tiss drove me to the match. I had Grandpa
George's scarf on and my pocket notebook ready
in my hand, but no new great football ideas ... YET.

"2, 4, 6, 8, WHO DO WE APPRECIATE? JOHNNY-
BEAR!" Mum clapped and cheered.

Now that we were a winning team, she wasn't

the only one making way too much noise. Yes, the number of Tissbury Primary fans was growing – and they were getting louder as well! Right, hand-shield up, football-focus on...

From the kick-off, Alex W tapped it to Tabia, who passed to Izzy, who ... PASSED TO BILLY! My dance-off plan had worked – Izzy's ball grog days were over! It was a miracle. Oh well, even if we lost 35–0, at least something good would have happened in the game.

But at half-time, we weren't losing badly. In fact, we weren't losing at all. We were winning 2–1, and Izzy had helped set up both goals, first for Alex "Koyo" W and then for Tabs. Tissbury were in dreamland and our ten supporters were going wild!

As I handed out the water bottles (Tabia had been right about that; apparently that was one of my assistant manager jobs), I was beaming with pride. If I didn't hate silly football phrases so much, I would have told them that they were all "playing out of their skins".

"YOU'RE ALL PLAYING OUT OF YOUR SKINS!" Mr Mann shouted.

But now that we were winning, wouldn't it be a good idea to have at least ONE defender on the pitch? No, not according to Mr Mann. Unfortunately, when I plucked up the courage to suggest a substitution, he was checking his phone, and Blether United were losing. Worst timing ever!

"OH, YOU KNOW BEST DO YOU, BALLY JUNIOR? I THINK YOU'LL FIND THAT I'M IN CHARGE HERE, AND WE'RE WINNING JUST FINE MY WAY!"

"Y-yes, sorry, Mr Mann."

But in the second half, Bartley attacked and attacked and attacked, until eventually – surprise, surprise – they scored (I told you so, Macho Mann!). Gabby rushed off her goal line and accidentally fouled their striker… Penalty! Billy tried his best to change the referee's mind, but it was no use.

"GO ON, GABBY – IT'S TIME FOR YOU TO SAVE THE DAY!" Mr Mann boomed.

I wasn't so sure about that. I had seen her save lots of penalties in training before, but this was different. Her legs were wobbling like jelly and it wasn't a dance move, or an attempt to put the striker off.

No, she was clearly super scared.

The penalty was pretty bad, but it didn't have to be good, because Gabby didn't even move. She couldn't. It was like her feet had grown roots way down into the ground. She just watched it fly straight past her and into the net. 2–2!

"Why didn't you DIVE for it?" Billy yelled at her. "That was such an EASY save!"

Uh-oh, Tissbury were in big trouble. There were still ten minutes to go, and Bartley were all over us like food on a baby's face. Forget the 1-2-1 or the 2-1-1; their new formation was just all four up front! What could we do?

"Think, Johnny, think!" I told myself on the touchline. Where were my great football ideas when I needed them? Tissbury would crash out of the County Cup, unless...

TING! LIGHT-BULB MOMENT – NO, LIGHTNING-BOLT MOMENT! Yes, yes, yes, it was going to be a great one, I could tell...

"CLARKY, ARE YOU READY?" Mr Mann said next to me.

Perfect! Not only could Alex C pass my message on to the others, but he would also have a massive part to play. Because, although Billy was the biggest kid in the school, he wasn't the best at headers. No, that was Alex C. He had a head like a hammer! Before he went onto the pitch, I talked him through the plan. For the second time that season, Grandpa George's extra-long scarf came in really handy.

When I laid it down on the grass in a zigzag shape, Alex C grinned. Good, he'd got it – I was giving him the chance to be the hero. "Coooool!" was all he said.

I also used my pocket notebook (thanks, Mum!) to write everything down for Alex C to give to Billy and Izzy and Tabs. They were key parts of the plan too. After reading it, Billy looked over and gave me a nod. A NOD! From Billy, that was about as rare as a leopard on a lilo.

Once everyone had taken up their positions, it was showtime. From the goal kick, Gabby played it to Izzy on the left,

who passed to Billy on the right,

who passed to Tabs on the left.

Zigzag, zigzag! Tissbury were weaving their way up the pitch, one pass at a time, and Bartley couldn't get back quickly enough.

It was time for the grand finale. Tabs curled a beautiful cross into the box and up jumped Alex C with his huge hammer head. 3–2 to Tissbury!

What a goal – Bartley had been hit by the Lightning Bolt! As everyone piled on top of each other, Tabia called me over to join in. And why not? I was the ASSISTANT manager, after all.

"YOU, JOHNNY BALL, ARE A FOOTBALL GENIUS!" she shouted and suddenly, for only the second time ever on a football pitch (that hat-trick, remember?), I was the centre of attention.

"Nice one, Johnny!"

"That was your greatest idea yet, mate!"

"Nice moves, DISCO BALL!"

Wait a second, was that – yes, that last voice belonged to Billy. First a nod and now four nice-ish words – blimey, Billy and I were basically friends!

Bartley tried their best to score again, but Tissbury were a proper team now. And it turned out that Mr Mann had been listening to me after all because he brought on Scott and Mo in defence.

"You ready, Super Sub?" I said, trying to smile as kindly as Mum does when I'm miserable.

"Super Sub" was my new nickname for Mo to try to settle his nerves. It seemed to be working. His face looked a healthy colour this time, and his voice didn't sound so shaky:

"Yes, Assistant Coach!"

Together, Mo and Scott defended our goal like Roman gladiators. The team held on until…

FWEEEET! Tissbury were the winners!

We celebrated like we'd just won the World Cup. Everyone was hugging and singing and dancing:

the Hip Wiggle,

the Butt Shake,

and, yes, you guessed it … the LIGHTNING BOLT!

Even Mum was dancing; no, especially Mum! I was having way too much fun to feel embarrassed, though. In fact, I was having the best time ever. I had finally found something that I was really good at. I was making friends and I was part of an awesome team. What could be better than that?

We were still one game away from the County Cup Final, but after beating Bartley, we felt like we could beat anyone.

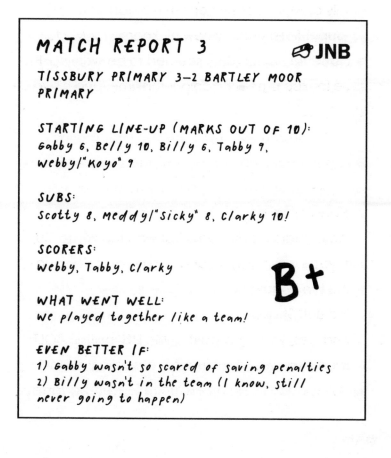

MATCH REPORT 3   ✏ JNB

TISSBURY PRIMARY 3–2 BARTLEY MOOR PRIMARY

STARTING LINE-UP (MARKS OUT OF 10):
Gabby 6, Belly 10, Billy 6, Tabby 9, Webby/"Koyo" 9

SUBS:
Scotty 8, Meddy/"Sicky" 8, Clarky 10!

SCORERS:
Webby, Tabby, Clarky

B+

WHAT WENT WELL:
we played together like a team!

EVEN BETTER IF:
1) Gabby wasn't so scared of saving penalties
2) Billy wasn't in the team (I know, still never going to happen)

"JUST" THE ASSISTANT MANAGER?

For the next week, our football team was the talk of the town. Well, the talk of the Tissbury Primary playground anyway. It was the biggest school news in years. We were through to the County Cup semi-finals for the first time S.D. (Since Daniel), and I was part of it.

When players look really happy after scoring amazing goals, silly football people say that they're "on cloud nine". But why only nine? We were on cloud 100,000,000!

I was feeling particularly pleased because:

1. (I don't like to boast but) my lightning bolt plan had worked BRILLIANTLY against Bartley.

2. I already knew my next assistant manager task – helping Gabby get over her fear of penalty kicks!

As we sat down for Saturday night football TV time, I was still buzzing about our victory. My family probably just wanted to watch *Match of the Day* in peace, but, for once, I had a story to tell.

"You should have seen their faces when Clarky scored – they looked so shocked, didn't they, Mum? It was like actual aliens had just landed on the pitch. I couldn't believe it either, but we did it – we're into the County Cup semis!"

"I'm so proud of you, pumpkin!" squealed Mum.

"Well done, son!" shouted Dad.

"Huh," snorted Daniel. My brother had been stomping around in a bad mood all day, because:

a) his football match had been cancelled

and

b) he was a teenager now and apparently that's what teenagers do.

Anyway, he'd had – and heard – enough of me.

"We, we, we – whatevs, bro, you don't even PLAY! Why are you getting so hyped? You're just the assistant manager!"

"Hey, that's not true! It was MY "sick" idea that helped us beat Lambert and MY *Koyo* plan that won the game against Shepherd's Cro—"

"Are you for real? Just listen to yourself, bro! Those aren't FOOTBALL ideas – they're stupid playground pranks. Even Macho Mann knows far more than you about football – he's just got you along for jokes!"

Well, that really burst my happy football bubble.

As I stormed upstairs to my bedroom, I could hear Mum and Dad telling him off.

"Daniel, what's got into you today? That wasn't nice! You know how much Johnny's enjoying being assistant manager!"

"Come on, son – why can't you just be happy for your brother? He's always happy for you!"

At first, I was really angry. What horrible things

to say! Of course I knew more about football than Mr Mann! And I was good at being an assistant manager! Was he jealous of me? Maybe he was worried that I was going to win the County Cup too, and he didn't want to share the glory!

I decided I wouldn't speak to my mean brother ever again...

But the more I thought about it, the more I had my doubts. Soon, I was playing a game of 20 questions:

1. Was Daniel right? Was I getting excited about nothing? Sure, I felt like I was helping, but I hadn't actually scored a goal, or even kicked a ball!

2. So, why was I walking and talking like a hero?

3. Was I just kidding myself, pretending I was part of the team?

4. Were my "great football ideas" really just "playground pranks"?

5. Was it actually Mr Mann who was making the difference, not me?

And on and on... For the first time since our County Cup run started, I wasn't so sure I wanted to be Tissbury Primary's assistant manager any more. Maybe it was time for me to hang up Grandpa

George's super-long scarf and use my pocket notebook for writing poems instead...

"No way, **WALRUS-WART!**" I could hear Tabia's voice in my head. "Johnny Ball, you're a football genius."

"Well, that's not what my brother thinks," I muttered miserably.

I looked around my room:

at my football-boot bed,

my football duvet cover,

my football posters,

my football lamp

and my football clock.

Daniel was right. Who was I kidding? I was no superstar; I was just the assistant manager for our school team. Everyone else probably thought I was a joke too. Was it time for me to just forget about football completely?

After a few more minutes, there was a KNOCK! at my door. I didn't say, "Come in!" but it slowly swung open anyway, and a head peered around...

Phew! It wasn't my evil brother; it was Mum. She came and sat next to me on the bed.

"How are you doing, dumpling?" she asked,

ruffling my hair until I shook her hand away.

"Mum, am I really just the 'assistant manager'?"

"No, not at all, angel! I'm sorry, Daniel shouldn't have said that. He didn't mean it, really! We're all very proud of you. And I've been to your matches. Your team needs you!"

"Really?"

"Really! What would they do without you? Lose every match, that's what! You're the brains behind their success, and you can't give up now. You've gotta do what you've gotta do!"

For that last line, Mum put on her awful American accent, of course. She might be super embarrassing sometimes, but she was always right. I couldn't give up now, not when we were only one game away from the County Cup Final. On his own, Mr Mann would ruin EVERYTHING!

No, I decided, Daniel would just have to get used to the idea that his little brother was Johnny Ball: Assistant Manager, "THE NEXT PAUL PORTERFIELD", and the future number one football genius in the whole wide world.

CHAPTER 13

WHO'S AFRAID OF A PENALTY KICK?

"What's on your mind, kiddo?" Dad asked me the next day as we took our seats at Railway Road Stadium for Tissbury Town vs Hawthorne Heath. Daniel was still sulking, so it was just the two of us at the game.

I guess I must have had my thinking face on.

I told Dad the truth. "Penalties."

What if our semi-final ended in a draw and went to a penalty shoot-out? Four scary spot kicks in a row – to Gabby, that would be worse than Halloween! She would probably run away, leaving an open goal behind her. No, I couldn't let that happen...

"A penalty kick?!" was Dad's reply when I explained. He was so shocked that he nearly spat out his pre-game Bovril. "Who's afraid of a penalty kick? When I was playing for the Tissbury Tigers,

I used to love a good shoot-out! Derek Dodds always knew that he could trust me to take the first one but then—"

"Yes, Dad; thanks, Dad," I said quickly before he could tell his right ankle story AGAIN. "But how can I show Gabby that penalty shoot-outs aren't so scary?"

"Well, Nigel could help you with that."

"Nigel?" I asked. Whenever I heard that name, I froze as still as a snowman. "Nigel who?"

"Nigel who?" Dad repeated like an angry parrot, actually spitting out his Bovril this time. Luckily, the seat in front was still empty. "How many Nigels do you know, son? I'm talking about Nigel Andrews, of course – old 'Hard Hands'!"

"Nigel who?" you're probably still thinking. Don't worry, a lot has happened since the start of this story, hasn't it? So, let me remind you: Nigel "Hard Hands" Andrews was Tissbury Town's Number One until he was 43 years old. He was so good in goal that he didn't even wear gloves. He was also so good that my parents decided to give me that middle name, but as I've already said, no one needs to know about the "Nigel".

"What a keeper he was!" Dad declared, doing his "happy memory" face. "He would still do a better job than this clown with finger-cushions," he said, pointing down at Tissbury's new Number One. "I only ever saw 'Hard Hands' let in one penalty, and that was because he was playing with three broken fingers ... all on the same hand!"

"That's great, but Gabby is already a good keeper, Dad. She makes lots of penalty saves in training. She just gets really spooked out in real matches."

"Well, 'Hard Hands' could help you with that too. The pressure was his favourite part of the job! In shoot-outs, he liked to play a fun game with the penalty-takers. He called it: "WHAT DO I HAVE TO DO TO MAKE YOU MISS?" Sometimes, he scuttled

across his goal from side to side like a crab; sometimes, he crawled across the grass, OINKING like a pig. Once, he even hung from the crossbar by his fingers like a monkey and saved the penalty with his foot!"

"Wow, do you think there would be videos of 'Hard Hands' online?" I asked. If Dad remembered him, he must be ancient!

"There must be something! We'll have a look when we get home..."

It turned out to be a super-fun day. First, we watched Tissbury thrash Hawthorne 5–1 ("The Rocket" scored a hat-trick!) and then Dad let me stay up REALLY late so we could watch every single "Hard Hands" video we could find.

"Thanks, Dad, you were right: he was AMAZING!"

Not only did I have my next great football idea, but for the first time ever, I felt proud of my middle name. Even Nigels could be football heroes! I decided right then that when I became "THE NEXT PAUL PORTERFIELD", the future number one football genius in the whole wide world, I would go by the name "Johnny N. Ball" (one step at a time!).

🏆 🏆 🏆

I couldn't wait to show Gabby all the videos of "Hard Hands", but WHEN and HOW? It was soon time for my second little white lie of the season.

"What can I do for you, Mr Ball?" Mrs Locke, the school secretary asked, looking down her long, posh nose at us. It was so long that we must have looked really small and far away, like light at the end of a tunnel.

"Miss Patel said that Gabby and I could use the computer room after school to look up some information for our homework. We're working on a project … in pairs … about the environment."

"I seeeeeeee," Mrs Locke replied really slowly. Were the words travelling all the way down her long nose?

It was a pretty good lie, but was it good enough to get past Mrs Locke? She guarded that computer room like it was a dragon's lair, so I decided to add a little extra detail.

"We're working on a campaign, you see. It's all about getting children to keep the school nice and clean."

"Oh, how excellent!" Mrs Locke said, handing over her precious computer room key straight away.

Phew, we were in! On the way to the computer room, I told Gabby about my plan. "Trust me, this is going to completely change the way you feel about penalties!"

"Penalties!"

Oh dear, just hearing the word made Gabby's legs wobble like jelly all over again. I could tell that this was going to be my toughest assistant manager mission yet.

"Sorry, I'll just call it 'The P Word' next time, I promise!" I said, quickly starting the video.

After a few minutes, I pressed pause on "Hard Hands".

"Look how much fun he's having!" I said to Gabby. "See, spot kicks aren't so scary for him, are they? That's because he turned penalty shoot-outs into an exciting game called: "WHAT DO I HAVE TO DO TO MAKE YOU MISS?" Keep watching – this next one's my favourite!"

As "Hard Hands" hung from the crossbar by his fingers, I looked over at Gabby. She was grinning like a turtle on a tyre swing.

"So, what do you think?" I asked her at the end. "Are you ready to play the game?"

Gabby shrugged. "Why not? I'll give it a go!"

The next day at training, the Tissbury players lined up ready for a practice penalty shoot-out.

On one team: Tabia, Mo, Alex C and Scott,

and on the other team: Billy, Alex W, Izzy and—

"BALLY JUNIOR!" Mr Mann boomed. "GET INVOLVED!"

I was expecting to hear jokes about balls, but there was nothing, not even a snort or a giggle.

"Cool, I can do this," I told myself. It was no big deal; I was only joining in with my team's training session. I just had to stay calm.

Gabby was thinking the same thing on her goal line. Eight opponents taking eight penalties – how horrible could it be? It was time for her to play: "WHAT DO I HAVE TO DO TO MAKE YOU MISS?"

At first, the answer to that question was "Try harder!" Once the ball was on the penalty spot, Gabby's fears seemed to come flooding back.

As Tabia stepped up, Gabby scuttled across her goal like a crab, but she was so nervous that she bumped straight into the post.

OUCH – GOAL! 1–0.

"Johnny, you get the BALL rolling for us!" Billy bellowed, pushing me forward.

As I ran up, Gabby tried to hang off the crossbar, but she was shaking so much that her fingers slipped, and she landed on her bum. I felt really bad for her, but at the same time, it gave me a great chance to score. Can I kick it? Yes, I can!

OUCH – GOAL! 1–1.

"Taxi for Gabby!" Billy bellowed and, of course, everyone else laughed. Now that he had their attention, he turned on me. Our brief moment of "friendship" was over. "Oi, Johnny, you call that coaching? You've made things worse!"

First Daniel and now Billy – why was everyone always so mean?

Mo was feeling much better now … GOAL! 2–1.

Alex W kicked it for Koyo … GOAL! 2–2.

After four penalties, Gabby hadn't saved a single one. My plan wasn't working at all. It was like watching a goalie horror show. But then I realized where she was going wrong.

"TIME OUT!" I shouted, making the "T" with my hands like I'd seen cool coaches do on TV.

"You don't have to copy all the Hard Hands

moves EXACTLY," I told Gabby. "You can do whatever YOU want, as long as you make them miss, OK?"

"Oh, OK!" she replied, looking a little less afraid.

Alex C ran up and ... Gabby started doing the can-can dance!

Right knee up, right leg KICK!

Left knee up, left leg KICK!

Alex C looked so confused, until Gabby somehow kicked herself in the face.

OUCH – GOAL! 3–2.

Izzy then had the easiest penalty of all. Gabby couldn't see a thing because she'd somehow poked herself in the eye with her big goalie-glove finger.

OUCH – GOAL! 3–3.

Billy wasn't the only one who was angry now; Mr Mann was about to explode. His big body was expanding with rage.

"BALLY JUNIOR, WHAT IS GOING ON? YOU'VE TURNED OUR KEEPER INTO A CIRCUS ACT!"

Uh-oh, if I didn't do something quickly, Mr Mann was going to kick me off the team and my coaching career would be over.

"I'm hopeless!" Gabby moaned, with only one eye open, like a pirate. "I might as well just stand here with both of my eyes closed. I've got more chance of catching a cold than a football!"

That's a good one! I thought. I'd never realized it before, but Gabby was actually really funny (way funnier than Billy, that's for sure)...

TING! LIGHT-BULB MOMENT – perfect timing! I quickly ran over and whispered my next great football idea to her.

The grin was back. "Cool, thanks, it's worth a try. I've got a whole joke book full of them!"

As Scott put the ball down on the penalty spot, Gabby looked up at him and said loudly, "Which football team loves ice cream more than you?"

"I dunno, who is it?"

Scott was laughing so hard that he could barely kick the ball.

ASTON VANILLA!

SAVED! As Gabby got up, she gave me a big goalie-glove thumbs up. Our plan was working!

It was time for the final penalty and Billy swaggered forward to take it. He had demanded to go last, just so that he could get all the glory. If he scored, we'd win the shoot-out.

"There's no point trying your rubbish jokes on me," Billy bellowed. "I know every joke ... EVER!"

Surely, Gabby would need a different plan to beat him? Billy only ever laughed at his own jokes anyway! But no, she wasn't giving up.

"Which football team should you never eat in a sandwich?"

Billy rolled his eyes like he'd heard it a million times before, but I could tell that he was only pretending to know it. He was curious. More curious than usual, anyway.

"It's LIVERpool, isn't it?" he guessed confidently.

Gabby shook her head.

"LEEKS United?"

Gabby shook her head again.

With each wrong answer, Billy grew more and more frustrated until finally, he'd had enough. "Whatever," he muttered angrily and then

HOOFed! the ball high over the crossbar.

CLANK! He MISSED!

Gabby threw her arms up triumphantly as Billy stormed off to collect the ball. She wasn't scared any more!

"So…" I started to say.

"So what?"

"You didn't finish your joke – which football team should you never eat in a sandwich?"

"Oh yeah, I forgot – OLD-HAM Athletic!"

As a wise man I call Dad once said, "A penalty kick? Who's afraid of a penalty kick?"

CHAPTER 14

A FOOTBALL IDEA TO FORGET

TISSBURY PRIMARY VS UPTON ACADEMY (PART I)

So, was that the end of Gabby's penalty panics? Did she go on to save the day for Tissbury? Not so fast – you'll have to keep reading if you want to find out!

For the first time, I woke up on game day feeling pretty good. We had made it to the County Cup semi-finals and the whole school was talking about us. We could hold our heads up high like heroes, even if Upton Academy crushed us like a can of lemonade.

There was one other important reason for my good mood: WE WERE GOING ON A ROAD TRIP!

That's right, Tissbury Primary were playing their first away game and that meant we would travel together, like a proper football team, like Tissbury Town. It also meant that Mum couldn't come to support us, so it was going to be far quieter too!

OK, so our school bus didn't have comfy seats and fancy gadgets, but, hey, who cares about that, right?* What mattered was: WE WERE GOING ON A ROAD TRIP!

*Wrong! Actually, it turned out that everyone cared about that apart from me.

"Sir, do we have to take the bus?" Billy groaned. "That thing looks like it's from Ancient Greece! It doesn't have WiFi, it doesn't have a TV screen and it'll probably break down anyway."

"Billy's right," said Tabia, for the first time ever. "If we arrive in that **WONKY-WAGON**, the Upton Academy kids are going to laugh their heads off. That school's so posh that I heard they've got their own private plane!"

"Last time I went in that bus, I threw up EVERYWHERE!" Mo warned.

UGHHHHHH!

But even that wasn't enough to change Mr Mann's mind.

"RIGHT, TROOPS, THAT'S ENOUGH OF YOUR UNGRATEFUL WHINING," he boomed. "WHAT DO YOU THINK THIS IS – A HOLIDAY? WELL, YOU'RE WRONG – THIS IS WAR! WE'RE LEAVING AT THIRTEEN

HUNDRED HOURS ON THE DOT. IF ANYONE'S LATE, THEY'LL BE LEFT BEHIND!"

"Thirteen hundred hours?" we all wondered; well, all except Scott.

"That's one o'clock," he explained to us. "My dad's in the army, and he says that's how they tell the time there. Twelve plus one, twelve plus two, twelve plus three—"

"OK, OK. We get it. STOP!" Billy shouted at Scott before it turned into another super-boring Maths lesson.

At 12.59 and 57 seconds, it was all-aboard the old school bus! Yes, apparently "timekeeper" was another one of my assistant manager jobs. Thankfully, however, Tabia had been wrong about the "driving the team bus" part.

That was Mr Mann's job and he took it very seriously. A little too seriously, if you ask me.

HONK! HONK!

"GET OUTTA THE WAY, YOU IDIOT!"

HONK! HONK!

"THE WAY YOU DRIVE, IT'D BE QUICKER TO WALK!"

HONK! HONK!

"GET A MOVE ON, YOU TWERP!"

Mr Mann's enormous egghead got redder and redder, until it looked like it might actually BOIL!

The journey was especially bad for me because I was sitting in the front seat. So, I had Mr Mann booming in one ear and the players moaning in the other.

"ARE WE THERE YET?"

"HOW MUCH LONGER?"

And at the same time, I was trying to find a song on the radio that everyone liked. Yes, apparently "DJ" was one of my assistant manager jobs too.

"BOOO, change it, Johnny – I hate that one!"

"Find 'Mr Funk Skunk'!"

"YAWN, boring – next!"

So, after all my excitement about GOING ON A ROAD TRIP, I was actually pretty glad when it was over. We made it through the Upton Academy gates with ZERO bus breakdowns and ZERO puking players. Success! Now, we just had to win a football match against one of the best school teams around. Easy!

"Legit" – that had been Daniel's one cool-kid-word reply when I asked him about Upton Academy. I didn't know what "legit" meant, but he'd nodded his head seriously, so I knew they must be really good. Oh well, what was the worst that could happen...?

Hailstones, no hailBOULDERS!

It had been raining all day, but just as we were about to get off the bus, the sky suddenly started sending down hailstones bigger than Koyo's flame-rocks, bigger even than Mr Mann's and Billy's heads put together!

I know there are lots of things worse than hailstones (dog farts, brain freeze, the plague, empty ice-cream tubs...) but it's still pretty bad, especially when your team is about to play a football match.

"LET'S GO, TROOPS – IT'S JUST A BIT OF RAIN!" Mr Mann boomed as the hailboulders pounded against the school bus roof. I know it sounds stupid, but it really felt like we were UNDER ATTACK! How could we stop Mr Mann from opening that door?

TING! MINI LIGHT-BULB MOMENT!

"Sir, do you think Blether United can win the league this season?"

That kept us on the bus for another fifteen minutes, but eventually, we had to make a run for the Upton Academy changing rooms.

Ready? 3, 2, 1, GO!

I'd never seen Billy move so fast, not even for the free burgers at the school summer barbecue.

As you can tell, we weren't exactly happy about the weather. But Upton Academy were FURIOUS!

"Look at the pitch," their coach wailed, as if it was a beautiful masterpiece that he had spent years painting. "It's a disaster!"

All of his clothes had the Upton school badge and the initials "PLT" on them – his trousers, his tracksuit top, his coat, even his hat (no, I didn't check his underpants). I know I can't really talk, with my "JNB" pocket notebook, but COME ON! Our players didn't even have the Tissbury school badge on their kits!

"I guess PLT must stand for Pretty Lame Teacher," Gabby joked.

Anyway, back to the pitch. Well, it wasn't really a pitch any more; it was a mudbath. A boggy, soggy, squelchy, spongy, slimy mudbath. Perfect for mud wrestling, TERRIBLE for football.

"RIGHT, TROOPS, DON'T BE AFRAID TO GET YOUR HANDS DIRTY TODAY!" Mr Mann boomed. "AND YOUR FEET, OF COURSE!"

Some of the other players weren't so sure, but Scott couldn't wait for kick-off. Messing around in the mud was his favourite thing in the world (even more than ice cream). He was famous for it at school.

WHEEEEEEEEEEEEEEEEEEEEEEEEE!

Scott shouted with every slide-tackle.

The Upton Academy players, however, really didn't share his love of getting dirty.

"My brand-new white boots!" their star striker moaned. "They're ruined! Mummy will be so mad with me."

His slick skills and fancy footwork were no match for Scott, the human toboggan. Tissbury were taking control.

Scott was completely covered in mud, from his old black boots all the way up to his smiling face. He was having the time of his life and his best game for Tissbury.

"THAT'S IT, LAD – THEY DON'T LIKE IT UP 'EM!" Mr Mann called out next to me.

Seeing Scott bossing the game should have made me feel better, but instead it made me feel nervous. Because suddenly, I was starting to BELIEVE. Yes, we could really do this – Tissbury could win this semi-final and go through to the County Cup Final!

But what could I do to help make that happen? I was determined to play my part and prove Daniel wrong. There was no "just" in "assistant manager"; I was the real deal! I could still hear my brother's mean words playing in my head: *Those aren't FOOTBALL ideas – they're stupid playground pranks.*

Even Macho Mann knows far more than you about football...

Maybe what I needed was a great idea that was a little more football-y and way less exciting. As I watched Scott's slides getting longer and longer, and closer and closer to our penalty area, I thought to myself, *What silly thing would football people like Mr Mann say right now?*

TING! TERRIBLE LIGHT-BULB MOMENT! And that's when I opened my big mouth and ruined everything: "Stay on your feet!" I called out. "Be careful, we don't want to give away any penalties."

I said that last word super quietly so that Gabby hopefully wouldn't hear. The last thing we needed was her getting spooked out by a spot kick.

Scott nodded, but I could tell that he was really disappointed. I was taking away his favourite football thing.

And that turned out to be a terrible mistake. The next time the Upton striker dribbled into the box, Scott was about to slide in as usual when he suddenly remembered my message. At the last second, he stopped and stood still, like he was playing stuck-in-the-mud. Before he could move,

the ball was in the back of our net.
1–0 to Upton!

My heart sank straight to the
bottom of my stomach, and I
buried my face in Grandpa
George's extra-long scarf.

"You just let him run right
past you!" Billy yelled at
Scott. "Why didn't you TACKLE him?"

Scott pointed straight at me and glared like his
eyes were lasers. I'd never seen him look so angry,
not even that day Mr Flake sold out of ice cream just
as he got to the front of the line.

And it wasn't just Scott who was angry with me; it
was the whole team.

"Nice one, SPITBALL!" huffed Alex C. "Now we're
going to lose the Cup because of you."

"I know you were only trying to help, Johnny," Izzy
tried to be kind, which was even worse, "but what
WERE you thinking?"

"LET THAT BE A LESSON TO YA, BALLY JUNIOR!" Mr
Mann said. "YOU DON'T KNOW BEST!"

I felt like the naughty dog who gets left outside in
the rain. Actually, that's pretty much exactly what I

was, only I didn't have the cute furry face to make them forgive me.

After being the hero against Bartley, I was now the Tissbury villain. They had been on their way to the County Cup Final until I stupidly tried to be the hero. Why couldn't I have just kept my big mouth shut? I was really kicking myself. I know what you're thinking – a Ball kicking himself! – but it really wasn't the time for jokes.

Even Billy could see that, but it WAS the perfect time for him to really bellow his worst words at me. It was like all his birthdays had come at once.

"Oh yeah, it's ALL your fault, Johnny! Keep your stupid football ideas to yourself next time! No one wants to hear them. You're just the assistant manager, and you're a rubbish assistant manager at that! We don't need you!"

For the first time ever, Billy was right; it was my fault. And Daniel had been right too; I was wasting my time, and now I was even making things WORSE for the team. Tissbury Primary would be better off without me and my foolish football ideas. Before I could say sorry, Mr Mann boomed: "THAT'S ENOUGH, BALLY JUNIOR – YOU'RE SACKED!

I WARNED YOU ABOUT THIS AND YOU DIDN'T LISTEN. YOU'VE GOT TOO BIG FOR YOUR BOOTS, BOY!"

Just when I'd thought things couldn't get any worse, I had been fired. I hadn't even been able to quit. I looked around at my team, feeling tears in my eyes. Mo? Alex W? Izzy? Surely, someone would stick up for me? I had helped each one of them, but no one said a word.

Tabia was my last chance. My best friend would have my back like always, wouldn't she? She, more than anyone else, knew what being the Tissbury Primary assistant manager meant to me. But no, my best friend just stared down at her boots and muttered, "Come on, let's get on with the game."

CHAPTER 15

ATTACK OF THE COMEDY KEEPER!

TISSBURY PRIMARY VS UPTON ACADEMY (PART II)

I'll be honest, that hurt like a paintball to the face. If Tabia wouldn't stick up for me, then I was officially on my own. I walked off and watched the rest of the first half from behind a tree near the car park. In no time at all, Tissbury were back in the match. Scott won the ball with, yep, you guessed it, a slide-tackle. He passed to Billy, who HOOFed! it to Alex W, who kicked it for Koyo. 1–1!

My team were better off without me. It was a sad end to the football adventures of Johnny Ball: Assistant Manager, but I only had myself to blame. I couldn't bear to watch any more. I stormed off to the school bus, lay down on the back seats and waited for it all to be over.

I lay there for ages, imagining Tissbury celebrating another amazing victory without me,

and trying to decide which after-school club
I would have to join instead of football (stamp
collecting, chess, bird-watching?). It must have
been less than 30 minutes, but it felt like a lifetime.

Then just when I was seriously thinking about
walking all the way home, there was a knock
at the window. Actually, it sounded more like a
BANG! and it wasn't just one; there were lots. Was
the bus under attack again?

"OK, OK – stop!" I sat up to see Tabia standing
there with a super-worried look on her face.

"Johnny, come quick!" she cried. "We need
you!"

I definitely didn't believe that last part, and
besides, I wasn't speaking to Tabia. There was
football and then there were best friends – best
friends always came first, no matter what. But
she had broken that golden rule, and so our best
friendship was over. In fact, she was the biggest
BOGEY-BRAIN-FART-FACE that I had ever met.

"Well, I'm not the assistant manager any more."
I folded my arms across my chest.

I waited for Tabia to leave, but she stood her
ground. Who would give in first?

Me, of course! Tabia always beat me at everything, plus I couldn't help being curious.

"Fine! What's happened then?" I asked.

"After you left, we fought back and equalized. Alex W scored—"

"I know, I was watching until half-time," I interrupted rudely. I wanted Tabia to know that I hadn't forgiven her that easily.

"Well, you didn't miss much in the second half. It finished 1–1 and now it's gone to..."

Penalties! Poor Gabby. I could see why Tabia was super worried now, but there was one thing that still didn't make sense.

"Wait, why are you here and not out there winning the shoot-out?"

Tabia crossed her arms and grunted. "Because Mr Mann subbed me off for Mo."

No way! What kind of a manager took their best player off just before penalties? I know I couldn't talk after my own terrible football idea, but even I wouldn't have done something that stupid.

"So, how's Gabby doing?" I asked, although I could already guess the answer.

"Not well at all. It's 2–2 so far. She's shaking like a

wet dog and she's doing the jokes, but she's getting them muddled. She needs your help, Johnny – WE need your help!"

"No, you don't," I said, shaking my head glumly. "I'll only make things worse, like I did with Scott."

"Hey, forget about that, **RAT-RASH** – we need you RIGHT NOW!"

I knew how much Tabia hated being wrong, but I was going to need more of an apology than that. "Well, it didn't look that way when you let Mr Mann fire me from the team!"

Could she say the magic word? That's all I wanted to hear, but it was as if Tabia's tongue was tied in a big, twisty knot.

"I'm–I'm really … SORRY, **SNAIL-SLIME**. There, I said it! I know I should have stood up for you, but I was angry. I mean, it was a bad idea telling him not to slide-tackle."

"Great, thanks for the reminder! It's the last time I ever listen to Daniel. I only did it because he said my football ideas were stupid playground pranks! And then Billy and Mr Mann—"

"Look, can't we talk about this later? We've got a County Cup semi-final to win! That was just one awful football idea vs a million great ones. Johnny, we both know you're a football genius and this is your big chance to show it. Come on!"

Although my brain said stay on the school bus, my feet followed Tabia back out onto the field. I was still mad at her, but I had to at least try to make up for my mistake...

We stopped to watch as Billy swaggered forward to take the next penalty, looking as confident as ever. This was his big chance to grab the glory! Last time, he had HOOFed! it high over the crossbar, but this time, he HOOFed! it high into ... top left bins. **CLANK!** 3–2 to Tissbury!

After a few loud cheers (mostly from Billy), the atmosphere got super-tense again. After all, this was a penalty shoot-out at the end of the County Cup semi-finals, and we were now one super save away from winning it. Now, that's nail-biting!

Some members of the Tissbury team looked pleased to see me again. Others, not so much.

"I hope you've come back to clear up your mess," Billy growled menacingly. "We'd have won by now if it hadn't been for Gabby's rubbish goalkeeping!"

"I'VE DECIDED TO GIVE YOU ONE LAST CHANCE, BALLY JUNIOR!" Mr Mann boomed, as if it was all his own idea. "NO MORE SCHOOLBOY ERRORS OR YOU'RE OUT!"

But I am a schoolboy! I thought to myself. There was no use arguing with Mr Mann, though. Especially not now.

The pressure had clearly got to Gabby. You know how some people start laughing when they're feeling nervous? Well, she was rolling around on the grass, cackling like a witch. I had to find a way to calm her down.

Think, Johnny, think!

Where were my great football ideas when I needed them? I didn't have much time; the Upton striker was pacing around impatiently. "Hurry up, you lot! I haven't got all day to be the hero!" he called out smugly.

Think, Johnny, think!

My plan had to be simple and successful. Otherwise, Mr Mann was going to squish me between his enormous hands. But even worse than that, Tissbury were going to crash out of the County Cup, unless...

TING! LIGHT-BULB MOMENT. Phew, just in time!

"Tabs, give me your water bottle," I said and then remembered my manners. "Please."

I needed a pen too, but I already had one of those so that I could write in my pocket notebook. Thanks, Mum! Weirdly, I was missing her a tiny bit.

As soon as I was ready, I raced over to get Gabby up off the grass and hand her the bottle. While she gulped down the water, I whispered in her ear: "Read the lid!"

Gabby was very confused at first, but then she looked down and saw the secret notes I'd written on the water bottle. Genius, right? They were the words to the greatest football joke in the world. Well, the only football joke that I could remember at that moment, anyway.

Gabby seemed to like

it, though. First, she smiled and then she laughed. This time, it wasn't a weird witch cackle like before; it was a real, proper laugh. Suddenly, she didn't look quite so scared any more.

"You've got this, G," I told her, sounding way more confident than I really felt.

You've got this, G? Wow, I was almost as super embarrassing as Mum! At least I hadn't tried an American accent, though.

"Thanks, J!"

As she stood in goal, there was a spring in Gabby's step again. She even banged her gloves together to show that she meant business.

"Finally!" the Upton striker huffed with his hands on his hips. "I'm going to be late for supper, thanks to you. And there's nothing I hate more than cold caviar!"

He placed the ball down, took a few steps back, and was just about to start his run-up, when:

"What do you do if you get too hot at a football match?" Gabby blurted out.

This was it: the big test. Would our comedy keeper plan work? Could she stay calm and win this massive game of: "WHAT DO I HAVE TO DO TO MAKE YOU MISS?"

Yes! The Upton striker was already answering!

"Hmm, well, when I go to watch matches with Daddy, we always bring a nice cold bottle of Fizzlebury's finest sparkling grape juice to share. But last time, security made us leave our ice bucket behind in the Range Rover! Can you believe it?"

Brilliant, the silly **FLAMINGO-FACE** hadn't even worked out that it was just a joke! He was clearly still thinking about his poor ice bucket as he ran up to take the penalty. His shot was good, but not good enough to beat GABBY "HARD HANDS" WALTERS...

SAAAAAAAAVED!

It was all over – Tissbury Primary were the winners! We were through to the County Cup Final, thanks to our Comedy Keeper.

"Yes, you LEGEND!"

"What a save!"

"THAT WAS A WORLDIE, GABBY!"

"Way to go, G!"

That last one was me, by the way, in case you hadn't guessed. We all bundled on top of Gabby and then carried her on a loud lap of honour around the pitch, chanting at the tops of our voices.

I was really relieved about making up for my
mistake, but there was still something missing … my
best friend. Who was I supposed to celebrate with
now? On the way back to the bus, Tabia walked
over to me slowly, like I was a wild animal who
might bite.

"W-well done, Johnny, I knew you could do it.
I'm–I'm really sorry that I ever doubted you. There,
did you hear that? I've said the S-word twice now,

PENGUIN-POO. So please forgive me, please! It won't happen again. Well, as long as you don't... Anyway, best friends for ever?"

I pretended to think about it for a few seconds.

"Best friends for ever!" I smiled, holding out my hand for our special, secret handshake.

As we left the school, the Upton Academy coach was still staring down at his tablet screen in disbelief. All his clever stats and graphs showed that they were by far the better team – so, how on earth had they lost?

I'll tell you how – because you can't beat a bit of humour! Sorry, Scott; I had learned my lesson the hard way:

FOOTBALL SHOULD ALWAYS BE FUN(NY).

"So...?" Billy said to Gabby on the now party bus back home.

"So what?"

"You didn't finish your joke – what DO you do if you get too hot at a football match?"

"Oh yeah, I forgot – SIT NEXT TO A FAN!"

"Nice one, Gabby!" Billy snorted like a satisfied bull.

"It wasn't my joke; it was Johnny's. He really

saved the day. I don't care what some of you say;
if you ask me, he's the BEST ASSISTANT MANAGER
EVER!"

MATCH REPORT 4   📣 JNB

TISSBURY PRIMARY 1–1 UPTON ACADEMY
(TISSBURY WON 3–2 ON PENS!)

STARTING LINE-UP (MARKS OUT OF 10):
Gabby 10, Scotty 9, Billy 4, Tabby 9,
Webby/"Koyo" 9!

SUBS:
Belly 9, Clarky 9, Meddy/"Sicky" 9

SCORERS:
Webby/"Koyo"

WHAT WENT WELL:
We made it to the County Cup Final!

EVEN BETTER IF:
1) I had let Scott carry on doing what he did
best (slide-tackling!)
2) Billy wasn't in the team (I know, still
never going to happen...)
3) Mr Mann wasn't the manager any more...

A

CHAPTER 16

JOHNNY BALL: ~~ASSISTANT~~ MANAGER

Don't worry, I knew that Gabby was just being nice.
I wasn't the "BEST ASSISTANT MANAGER EVER".
Right then, I wasn't even in the Top 200 Million!

But at least I had my best friend back and the
Tissbury players weren't angry with me any more.
On the party bus, I was getting high-fives and hugs
from everyone*, even Scott.

"We all slip up sometimes," he said, still wearing
his mud mask. "You know me; I do it all the time!"

*Well, not Billy, obviously, but that would have
been way too weird anyway.

By the time I got home, I was feeling a lot better
about myself, but I still had DOUBTS. I couldn't talk
to Daniel any more. Since our fight, he was walking
past me as if I was his invisible brother. So instead, I
decided to make a worry list, just like Miss Patel had
taught us in class:

~~WORRY~~ DOUBT LIST

Will Mr Mann listen to my football ideas ever again?

Will the Tissbury players trust my football ideas ever again?

Is Daniel right that being "just" the assistant ~~manager is a waste of time anyway?~~

Is Billy right that I just make things worse?

Am I good enough to even be Tissbury Primary's ~~assistant manager, let alone~~ "THE NEXT PAUL PORTERFIELD", and the future number one football genius in the whole wide world?

Writing my doubts down definitely helped. I could have kept going, but I had reached the end of the page, and I didn't want to fill up my pocket notebook before ...

THE COUNTY CUP FINAL!

Tissbury would be playing in the final for the first time S.D. (Since Daniel) and that was a super-huge achievement. It was the main reason why I had been so happy to become the assistant manager in the first place. That, and making my football family proud of me, and maybe I could still achieve that too, even with my brother. I couldn't give up now. There was a chance that my team might need my (mostly) great football ideas one last time.

So, I worked harder than ever to find a way for us to win that County Cup. Remember, I had been dreaming about that moment for years: the party, the pride, the glory, the winners' medal and, of course, that glittering trophy. With that image to inspire me, I scribbled down lots of great ideas for training exercises, just in case Mr Mann let me do some actual coaching at our last team practice before the big day...

🏆 🏆 🏆

"RIGHT, TROOPS, I'VE GOT SOME GOOD NEWS AND SOME BAD NEWS," he boomed once we were all huddled together on the field, ready for training. "I'LL START WITH THE BAD NEWS – SADLY, I WON'T BE THERE AT THE COUNTY CUP FINAL..."

That was the BAD news?! HURRAY! On the outside, I tried my best to look super sad but, on the inside, I was jumping with joy.

"NOW FOR THE GOOD NEWS – THE REASON THAT I WON'T BE AT THE COUNTY CUP FINAL IS BECAUSE I GOT A CALL FROM BLETHER UNITED LAST NIGHT.

THEY'VE BEEN WATCHING MY SUCCESS HERE, AND THEY WANT ME TO BE THEIR NEW MANAGER!"

Wait, WHAT? How? Why? When? Blether United wanted Mr Mann? No way! There had to be a mistake! At first, I didn't know what to say, but eventually, I went for:

"Congratulations, Sir. I'm so happy for you!"

(*And for me!* I thought, but I made sure that I only thought it.)

"THANKS, BALLY JUNIOR, IT'S A DREAM COME TRUE. IT FEELS LIKE ALL MY HARD WORK HAS FINALLY PAID OFF! I KNEW I HAD A TOP FOOTBALL BRAIN, BUT I NEVER THOUGHT I'D GET THE CHANCE TO USE IT..."

Was Mr Mann about to cry? His eyes were wetter than Billy's trousers that time in nursery...

"So, who'll be our manager for the final, Sir?" Tabia asked. Then she looked at me and we both crossed all our fingers and toes.

"WELL, I'LL DECIDE THE TEAM AND THE TACTICS..."
What tactics?

"...AND THEN BALLY JUNIOR WILL BE THERE ON THE SIDELINES. DON'T LET ME DOWN, TROOPS!"

Wow! Me? The Tissbury Primary manager for the County Cup Final? What a day to make my debut!

My face didn't know what to show first: happiness, pride or total panic.

HAPPINESS

PRIDE

TOTAL PANIC

I looked around at my team, just like I had after my awful mistake against Upton. This time, they weren't glaring at me; they were smiling. Well, most of them anyway.

But what about all my DOUBTS? What if I made another awful mistake in the final? Could I really do this? There was only one way to find out...

Oh boy, things were moving way faster than I'd thought. A few weeks ago, I had started out as Johnny Ball: Assistant Manager. Now I was Johnny Ball: FOOTBALL Manager already! Then, if we won the County Cup Final, I would be on my way to becoming Johnny N. Ball, "THE NEXT PAUL PORTERFIELD", and the future number one football genius in the whole wide world!

"Calm down, calm down." I stroked my excited brain like it was a soft, furry cat.

I had to take things one step at a time. As Grandpa George would say, I still had wallops of work to do. Especially as one player in particular was furious about Mr Mann's big news. Can you guess who?

CHAPTER 17

BILLY'S BOOTS

"WHOA, WHOA, WHOA!" Billy yelled, barging his way to the front of the team huddle. "You've got to be kidding, Sir! You're leaving the BALL BOY in charge for the County Cup Final, the biggest game of all? We've got no chance now! Have you forgotten the mess he made against Upton?"

"Shut it, *GOOSE-GRIN*. That was one mistake!" It was Tabs who said it, but I was thinking it too. "Johnny knows what he's doing. He's already shown that he's full of great football ideas!"

"Yeah!" shouted Scott.

"Yeah!" yelled Mo.

"KOYO!" added Alex W.

"Yeah!" roared Izzy.

With each cheer, my heart leaped higher and higher like it was on a trampoline. This time, the Tissbury players were sticking up for me!

"Yeah!" cried Gabby. "I can barely manage to get out of bed in the morning, but Johnny can definitely manage our football team!" Wow, they trusted me again too!

That left one last player – Alex C. Whose side was he on? On the one hand, I had helped him and his hammer head to become the heroes against Bartley Moor. But on the other hand, his best friend, Billy, was glaring at him so hard that it looked like he might burn a big hole in the back of Alex C's head...

At first, I thought Alex C was just mouth-breathing, but actually, he was mumbling words. "Leave it, mate, Johnny's ... OK."

"Johnny's OK" – it wasn't exactly Mum-level praise, but Billy didn't see it that way. He stormed off like Alex C had just called me "THE NEXT PAUL PORTERFIELD" or something.

"Whatever, I'm done with this stupid school team, anyway. I QUIT, BALL BOY! Good luck in the final without me!"

Uh-oh. The players had already been feeling nervous about the County Cup Final, but this would make them properly panic. When I looked around, all eyes were on me, including Mr Mann's. What, was I supposed to solve this? I guess this was what being a proper manager was like.

"Don't worry, I'll talk to him," I told them, trying to sound less worried than I felt. Finally, my wish to have a team without Billy had come true. But now, I wasn't so sure it was what I wanted. We had come so far together, and we couldn't lose our captain now, just before our biggest game.

As I arrived at the changing room door, Billy was making a lot of angry noise.

"Those thud-heads won't win anything without me – I'm their captain!" he bellowed. "I hope they get THRASHED!"

Meanwhile, he was flinging his football kit all over the floor. First, one shin pad, and then the other:

CLATTER! CLATTER!

Then one gleaming golden
boot, and then the other:

CLANK! CLANK!

There was that special sound again, but Billy
hadn't even HOOFed! a ball! He was also grunting
like a pig, like the boots were really heavy. Wait a
second – what if they weren't just gold coloured?
What if they were actually MADE OF GOLD? I had
to find out...

"Billy, I'm really sorry if we've upset you," I said.
"We need you back – you're our leader!"

As much as I hated to admit it, it was true. When
he wasn't too busy being a big bully, he was
actually a pretty good footballer. He wasn't Tabia-
good – no way! – but he was still our second-best
player. With the right coaching, his HOOF! could be
a really dangerous weapon.

"Whatever, BALL BOY. Just leave me alone!"

I pretended I was tidying up, but really, I just
wanted to get a closer look at his boots...

"Hey, don't touch them!" Billy said.

Too late – the left one was already in
my hand.

No, they weren't made of gold. But they were still way heavier than any boots I had ever seen, even the super ancient ones at Tissbury Football Museum. Oof! One boot weighed as much as all of Daniel's football trophies combined!

No wonder Billy never did any running! It was amazing that he could even lift his feet high enough to HOOF! the ball.

"Where did you get these?" I asked.

"None of your business!" Billy replied, snatching it back. "I'm not talking to you – you're trying to ruin MY football team!"

"No, I'm not! I deserve that manager job, whatever you say!" I told him, standing up for myself for once. I had finally found something that I was really good at, and I wasn't giving up now. "Look, can't we just work together? We've only got one more match to go!"

"Yeah, and you're going to mess it up … AGAIN!"

"I don't understand; I thought things were good with us after the Bartley game. And I made up for that mistake against Upton, didn't I? So, what's your problem now?"

There was silence while Billy snarled for a bit. That was his way of thinking of the meanest things to say.

"You, BALL-BRAIN – you're my problem!" he said eventually. "You keep helping all the others to become heroes, but what about ME? I know I'm playing brilliantly…"

REALLY???

"…but I haven't scored any goals yet! Well, other than that perfect penalty against Upton…"

"Well, those hulking-great golden boots aren't helping!"

That's what I wanted to say, but there was no use arguing with Billy. And by now, I had learned that it wasn't always good to say exactly what I was thinking. I had to do what was best for the team; I was the manager now.

So, how could I persuade Billy to come back? By giving him the chance to be Tissbury's star player, the centre of attention. He didn't seem like someone who needed a confidence boost, but a little more couldn't hurt, could it?

"Exactly! You've been playing so well that I didn't

think you'd want my help," I explained. "But don't worry, I've saved a super-great football idea for you – the greatest of them all! You're going to be our County Cup Final hero!"

"Really?" Billy asked me.

Really? I asked myself. Why had I said that? Now I'd have to come up with something special!

"Go on then, what's the plan?" he asked.

"I-it's not quite … you'll, err, have to wait until match day. Come on, let's get back to training. We've got a final to prepare for!"

Billy nodded and started putting his gleaming gold boots back on. No, no, no! I had to get rid of those massive monsters, but how?

TING! MINI LIGHT-BULB MOMENT.

"Here, why don't you try these?" I said, handing him my old pair. "Daniel loved those boots, but they don't fit him any more."

Billy was about to say, "No way!" until he heard the Tissbury magic word: "Daniel." After that, those boots were on his feet in a flash.

"Cheers, these feel … different," Billy admitted as he ran back onto the pitch.

I bet they do! I thought to myself. It must have

felt like walking across a field of Mr Flake's ice cream.

The other players looked very relieved to see us returning together. Phew, it was a miracle! I had passed my first test as Tissbury Primary's manager. Now the practice could begin.

Billy's HOOF! wasn't quite so hard any more, but at least he wasn't weighed down. Now, he could use his power and strength to run around – well, a bit anyway.

"THAT'S IT, BILLY," Mr Mann shouted. "I WANT TO SEE YOU ALL RUNNING THROUGH BRICK WALLS FOR THE TEAM!"

It was our last practice before the County Cup Final, and we should have been working hard on EVERY PART OF OUR GAME PLAN:

our fitness,

our tactics,

our tackling,

our passing,

our shooting,

defending corners and free kicks

and attacking corners and free kicks...

But what were we doing instead? Yep, you guessed it – we were just playing a match!

I wanted to say something to Mr Mann – I really did – but what if he got angry again and decided to take away my manager job? No, I couldn't let that happen, so I kept my great football ideas to myself ... for now.

Anyway, back to Billy. Sadly, a new pair of boots wasn't going to solve the biggest problem of all: his awful attitude.

"Get back, you bozo! It's not my fault you can't control my perfect pass."

"It's like playing with a bunch of football fools!"

"Scott, if you slide-tackle me one more time,

I'm going to HOOF! that ball in your face!"

Billy was meant to be the team leader, but he certainly wasn't acting like it. He was fighting with absolutely everyone! As Tabia trudged off the pitch, she lasered me with a look that said:

"DO SOMETHING!"

She was right. I had to put a stop to Billy's awful attitude, but how? How could I make sure that he was on his best behaviour for the final?

Take away the captain's armband? No, that might make him even angrier!

Tell him that Daniel would be there watching? No, that might make him show off even more!

TING! MAJOR LIGHT-BULB MOMENT.

Of course! Who was the person that Billy was most scared of in the whole wide world?

HIS MUM!

No one messed with Mrs Newland. I had learned that lesson at nursery when I'd accidentally run over her foot with my tricycle. Never again!

But if it could help Tissbury to win the County Cup Final, then I would do it. I would speak to Billy's mum and make sure that she was there watching.

CHAPTER 18

A SCARY SCOUTING ADVENTURE

There was one other person that I wanted to visit before the big day.

"How's my favourite little follyflop?"

"I'm good thanks, Grandpa George. No, actually, I'm better than good – I'm GREAT! Mr Mann can't make the County Cup Final because he says he's going to be the new Blether United manager. And best of all, he's left me in charge!"

"Oh, that's fantiddlytastic news! Well, it's luverly luck that I have another scarf to wear then, isn't it? I'll just need to remember where I left it..."

"Wait," I nearly spat out my milky tea, "you're coming to the final, Grandpa?"

"Why, I wouldn't miss it for the woly-poly world!"

Oh boy, my big day was getting bigger and bigger. What if we got hammered, like Billy had said? That would be even more super embarrassing with Grandpa George watching as well as my super-embarrassing mum! But it was my job to make sure that didn't happen.

"So, do you feel ready? Did you have to do all your research in a rabbity old rush?"

"What 'research', Grandpa?"

"Learning all the important thingymanoodles. Before any big match, Malcolm McCleary, that mean magubbin, would send me out to spy on our opponents, whatever the wurly weather."

"And did it help?"

"Sometimes, it really saved our bacon, and other times, it didn't make a tiddly bit of difference. Still, it likely led to a light-bulb moment or three for me!"

Really? That would be super helpful, but wasn't it cheating? I didn't want to break the rules to beat Epic Forest in the final, but at the same time, it would be useful to see just how "epic" they really were...

That night, I couldn't sleep for ages because questions were going around and around my head like annoying brain boomerangs.

By the morning, I had almost made up my mind. But if I really was setting off on a scary scouting adventure, I wasn't going on my own. No, I needed my best friend by my side.

"That's a great football idea, Johnny!" Tabs seemed way more excited than me. "I've got a friend who goes to Epic, so I know how to get there. They practise on a Thursday, I think ... hey, that's today. Let's go!"

"OK ... we're really going to do this?"

"Come on, don't be such a **SWEET-CHILLI-CHICKEN**, Johnny. We're doing it for Tissbury, remember, and you're our manager now!"

Tabs was right. There was no time to be a sweet-chilli-chicken; we had a County Cup Final to win. So, after school, we climbed on board the number 52 bus and set off on our scary scouting adventure.

"What's our plan once we get there?" I asked as we sat down on the top deck.

"Don't ask me," Tabs replied, "you're the one with all the great football ideas!"

Why did I always have to think of everything? I tried not to panic or pick a nasty name battle with her.

"What if we just pretend that we go to Epic?" I asked.

Tabs shook her head. "You know what Mrs Locke's like at our school. I bet they know everyone's name there too!"

Good point.

"OK, what if we pretend that we've got brothers and sisters who go to Epic? We could pick two really popular names like ... Alex ... and Emma."

But Tabs shook her head again. "Don't even try

to fool ladies like Mrs Locke, Johnny. We'll have to find another way in!"

The only other way in turned out to be climbing over the fence behind the Epic football pitch. It wasn't actually that high but, as we stood in front of it, it towered over us like a mountain.

Honestly, I've never been so nervous in all my life. What if someone spotted us trying to climb it? I looked left, then right, then left, then right, as if I was crossing a really busy road at home time.

"All clear!" I whispered.

Tabs went first. She clambered up the fence and landed her jump like a pro. I, on the other hand, well, I can be quite clumsy sometimes.

"Just take it slowly," Tabs told me, as I started to climb, but my legs were shaking, and that was making the fence wobble beneath my feet.

WHOAAAAA!

Before I knew what was going on, I landed palms down in the mud.

SNIFF! SNIFF! UGHHHHH!

No, it wasn't mud on my hand, after all; it was a dirty, stinking fox poo! I found some big leaves to wipe it away, but it was still there. I could smell it!

"Focus," Tabs said, shaking me like a vending machine with something stuck inside. "We're doing this for Tissbury, remember!"

She was right, as always. We had to find a way to win the County Cup Final. We crept forward as far as we could – watching out for any more "surprises" along the way – and then found a spot behind some big bushes to spy on Epic's training session.

So, what did we learn from our scary scouting adventure? Well, Epic were definitely epic at football. Every single one of their players could:

HOOF! the ball like Billy (with his gold boots on!), hammer-head it like Alex C, slide-tackle like Scott

AND show off MAD SKILLZ like Tabs.

Even their goalie!

We're doomed, I thought miserably, but I didn't say that to Tabs. I didn't need to. She could see it with her own eyes.

Plus, their coach was clearly a million times better than Mr Mann; no, a zillion! She didn't boom out silly football phrases like an action figure.

Instead, she said normal things that made sense. That was my kind of manager! Her football brain was so big that there can't have been much room for anything else. I scribbled down as much as I could in my pocket notebook: words, drills, tactics. There was so much more for me to learn!

It was only right at the end of the practice that Epic played a proper football match. And, boy, were they brilliant!

PASS, THEN MOVE,

PASS, THEN MOVE,

PASS, THEN MOVE – GOAL!

But just when I was giving up all hope of ever winning the County Cup Final, I spotted something interesting.

The three girls on Epic's team had been super good during the drills, but in the match, they barely got a chance to touch the ball. Even when they were standing in lots of space, the boys just passed to each other instead.

When the coach blew her whistle for a drinks break, the players formed two different groups on the pitch:

the boys on one side

and the girls on the other.

Interesting… It was especially interesting to me because our best player was a girl – Tabs! If the Epic boys were stupid enough to think that they were better than girls, then she would happily prove them wrong, with a little help from her teammates, both the boys and the girls…

TING! LIGHT-BULB MOMENT. I had Miss Patel to thank for this one. In class, we had been learning all about Ancient Greece: the gods, the togas, the Olympics and … THE TROJAN HORSE.

The Trojan Horse was my new favourite story EVER. Basically, those greedy Greeks really wanted to take over a city called Troy, but they couldn't find a way in (a bit like me and Tabs at Epic Forest).

So what they did was leave an enormous wooden horse outside the city gates. Don't ask me why, but the silly Trojans took one look at it and thought, *Wow, thanks, what a lovely gift!*

Then, when they brought the horse into the city and went to bed ... TA-DA! It turned out that the enormous wooden horse was full of super-strong Greek soldiers.

Great idea, right? But what if I could turn it into a great football idea? What if we, Tissbury Primary, could take our own Trojan Horse to the County Cup Final? Not a real horse, obviously, or a wooden one either. No, just a super-clever plan to trick those silly Epic boys...

But just as I was working it all out in my head, something REALLY scary happened. Suddenly, we could hear a super-loud, wailing siren sound and the words:

"INTRUDER ALERT! INTRUDER ALERT!"

Uh-oh, we must have somehow set off Epic's security alarm climbing over the fence! The training session stopped immediately, and the players spread out to search for the intruders.

"I bet it's those twerps from Tissbury, coming to spy on us!"

"If so, let's show them how serious we are about keeping our training sessions secret!"

Nooooo! My worst nightmare was coming true. Once they caught us, Tissbury would be kicked out of the County Cup, ALL BECAUSE OF ME...

"Come on, let's go back the way we came!" Tabs whispered to me, but it was no use. We wouldn't make it over the fence in time.

Think, Johnny, think! It was now or never...

TING! ANOTHER LIGHT-BULB MOMENT.
Phew, my football brain was on fire!

"No, follow me!" I told Tabs quietly, pointing towards the pitch.

"What? Are you crazy?"

"No, I'm not; I promise!"

Together, we raced out onto the grass, which was now empty because the coach and all of the players were searching for us in the bushes.

"Quick, grab one of their hoodies!" I said, snatching one for myself too. It wasn't stealing; it was just borrowing. We would bring them back later.

Soon, we were walking calmly (well, sort of) past the Epic Forest school office, with "EPIC" written on our backs and our hoods right up. It was a pretty good disguise, but would anyone notice us...?

No! We walked as far as the school gate, then left the hoodies there and ran away as fast as we could.

🏆 🏆 🏆

"I'm never ... doing ... that ... again!" I panted as we sat down on the back seat of the bus.

This time, Tabs didn't call me a sweet-chilli chicken. I think even she was too terrified for a nasty name battle right then.

But the good news was that, thanks to our scary scouting adventure, I now knew what my super-clever County Cup plan would be.

CHAPTER 19

TISSBURY'S TROJAN TABIA

TISSBURY PRIMARY VS EPIC FOREST (PART I)

OK, that's enough of the boring build-up. It's time to fast forward to the main event – THE COUNTY CUP FINAL!

That morning, I was feeling way too nervous to sit down and enjoy my usual "Three-a-Fried" breakfast. But Mum wouldn't stop talking:

"Aren't you the cleverest little clog?"

"Would you like to see the smart new coat I bought you for your big day?"

"And this nice waistcoat! All the top managers are wearing them these days…"

No, no and no (thanks)! I already had everything that I needed: my scarf, my pocket notebook and my head full of great football ideas … hopefully!

I got Dad to drop me off super early so that I could have some time alone to think. As Tiss drove out of the car park, Dad flashed his lights to wish me luck. I was going to need it. I was about to experience my first proper match as a football manager, and if I failed, it might be my last. As I stood there on the touchline, the empty pitch looked enormous. I tried to imagine the game going on in front of me:

What would I say?

What would I DO?

Think, Johnny, think!

One by one, the Tissbury players arrived, and I could tell that they were just as nervous as me.

Gabby's legs were shaking like someone had just shouted, "PENALTIES!"

Mo looked like he was going to be sick again.

Alex W was so quiet that I thought someone had told him that Koyo wasn't real.

Uh-oh, what they needed was a TOTALLY AWESOME TEAM TALK! What was I going to say? Think, Johnny, think!

"Right, troops," I started, but then I stopped straight away. I didn't need to do my best mini-Mr-Mann impression any more. I was free to be me – Johnny Ball: Football Manager, "THE NEXT PAUL PORTERFIELD", and the future number one football genius in the whole wide world!

I cleared my throat and started again:

"Today's match is going to be super tough, but there's nothing to be nervous about, I promise. Just enjoy it, because you've done so well to get this far. Epic Forest are ... epic, but you're epic too, OK? I believe in you all. Look what you've achieved already by working together as a team!"

"YEAH!" cheered everyone except you-know-who.

"Billy, is there anything you want to say as captain?" I asked.

Tabs looked at me like I'd just beaten her in a nasty name battle. What? Why? A battle cry from Billy sounded like the worst football idea ever...

"If it wasn't for me—" Billy began to bellow, but before he could finish, he spotted someone standing near by. It was like he'd been hit in the face by one of his own heavy metal boots (he was now wearing Daniel's old ones instead, thankfully!).

"Mu-mu-mu-mum, what are you doing here?"

"Is that any way to greet your mother? Your manager invited me, William. He said this game was important, but I suppose it must have slipped your mind to tell me."

"M-m-m-mr Mann?"

"No, Mr Ball actually, but we'll discuss exactly what he had to say later. Just get on with your speech, William – your team is waiting. 'If it wasn't for me'...?"

Suddenly, Billy was on his best behaviour. "I-i-if it wasn't for me-ETINGS like this, we wouldn't be such a strong team. Well done, everyone, let's win this final!"

At first, the others were too shocked to say anything, but soon they were cheering again. "YEAH!"

I looked down at the long list in my pocket notebook:

Get Billy to play nice – TICK!

So far so good. On to Step Two of my County Cup Final master plan...

"I know Mr Mann named the team at practice, but I'm going to make one tiny change," I announced. "Billy, I want you to move back into defence and, Scott, I want you to move forward into midfield. OK?"

Billy checked to see if his mum was still watching; sadly for him, she was. "OK," he muttered moodily.

Well, that was easy! Step Three could wait until after kick-off.

🏆 🏆 🏆

FWEEEEEEET!

I had never seen so many people turn up for a Tissbury Primary match before. There were loads of fans that I didn't even know, and some that I definitely did:

"YOU CAN DO IT, JOHNNY-DEAREST!"

"Go on, son, show them how to – owwwww, my ankle!"

"Bravo, miladdy – absatootly razzle-dazzle!"

And Daniel. What was my brother doing there? We still weren't speaking, so had Mum and Dad forced him to come? Whatever the reason, he stood as far away from our family as possible, not saying a single cool-kid word and probably wishing that he could have stayed at home instead.

It was great to see them all there watching, but I had wallops of work to do. Hand-shield up, football-focus on…

One of the silliest things that football people say is: "It's a game of two halves."

Well, duh? But actually, the County Cup Final was more like a game of three thirds. In the first, Tissbury were definitely the team on top.

Gabby "Hard Hands" Walters saved every Epic shot.

Billy looked way better in defence, where he didn't have to run so much and he could HOOF! the ball even harder.

Scott sprinted around the midfield, sliding into every tackle like it was a puddle of mud.

Alex W looked ready to kick it for Koyo.

And Tabia ... well, actually Tabia was playing really badly. It was like she had flippers instead of feet!

"What wa—" Billy began to shout at her until he remembered who was watching.

"—rm weather! Perfect for a Cup Final."

Don't worry, Tabia was only doing what I'd told her to do – "play really badly". That was Step Three of my County Cup Final master plan. You'll see why in a second...

Epic looked good, but not ... epic. The boys passed and then moved, passed and then moved, but the girls just moved ... and moved ... and moved. They barely got a touch of the ball, just like we'd seen on our scary scouting adventure.

"Pass it to Priya!" their coach kept calling, but it was as if the Epic girls were invisible.

And after a few of her most terrible touches, Tabia was almost invisible too.

"Don't worry about marking her," I heard the silly Epic boys say. "She's not their danger MAN!"

I couldn't wait to see my best friend run rings around them. I gave her the signal – it was time for … TISSBURY'S TROJAN TABIA!

The next time she got the ball out on the left wing, her flippers had miraculously turned back into mad-skilful feet! Uh-oh, those Epic boys were in big trouble. Just like the Trojans, they hadn't spotted the danger (WOMAN!) until it was way too late.

Cruyff Turn.

Rainbow Flick.

Stepover 1, stepover 2, stepover 3…

Nutmeg.

GOOOOOOOOAAAAAAALLLL!!!!!

Wow, it was even better than I'd expected! The Epic boys rubbed their eyes like they'd just seen a unicorn, and the Epic girls just clapped … and clapped … and clapped.

"THAT'S MY GIRL," Mum shouted in her awful

American accent, "AND MY BOY TOO!"

I raced down the touchline with both arms up in the air. I couldn't help it – my master plan had worked and Tissbury were winning the County Cup Final!

"Wait, was that all part of the plan?" Billy bellowed, looking as confused as an elephant on ice.

"That's right," Tabia cried out triumphantly. "Johnny Ball, have I ever told you that YOU'RE A FOOTBALL GENIUS?"

DIVING'S FOR ... DINGBATS!

Tissbury Primary vs Epic Forest (Part II)

Hopefully by now you're on Team Tissbury, just like me. Did you celebrate Tabia's wonder-goal with a **WHOOP!** and a special, secret handshake? Well, if you did, don't get too excited just yet.

Because remember what I told you a few pages ago? The County Cup Final was a game of three thirds. The first third belonged to us, but sadly the second third belonged to Epic.

Two things happened that changed the game completely:

1. Their coach took off one of the silly boys and brought on another girl.

2. Epic became ... epic!

PASS, THEN MOVE,

PASS, THEN MOVE,

PASS, THEN MOVE...

Normally, I love watching fantastic, flowing football like that, but not when I'm the manager of the other team! What could I do to stop them? If I didn't do something soon, Epic were going to pass us right off the pitch!

Think, Johnny, think!

Scott was doing his best to win the ball back, but it was like a game of piggy-in-the-middle and he was the poor little piggy.

"I need some help here!" he called out.

"Do your own de—" Billy began to bellow, but luckily for him, he didn't even have the energy to finish his sentence.

Somehow, we made it through to half-time without letting in a goal. Phew! We were still winning the County Cup Final. But as the Tissbury players walked off the pitch, they looked more like zombies than footballers. They were so exhausted that they could hardly put one foot in front of the other.

"Come on, team, we're halfway there!" I told them, but Alex W was slumped on the ground and Scott wasn't moving.

"Izzy and Mo – get ready. You're coming on!"

"Yes, Coach!"

"YES, COACH – I'M READY FOR THIS!"

"That's it, Super Sub!"

I had never seen Mo look so calm and determined about football. He sprang to his feet with his fists clenched and started doing some stretches. He certainly wasn't "Sicky" any more.

I looked at the rest of my team. Gabby could carry on in goal, Billy didn't do much running anyway, and Tabs didn't know the meaning of the word "tired". Good, all set for the second half!

But first, it was time for my TOTALLY AWESOME HALF-TIME TEAM TALK. It was going to have to be the greatest speech of my life:

"Listen up, this is your big chance to go down in Tissbury Primary history. In years to come, people will be talking about you like they talk about Daniel now!"

That glorious name was enough to wake Billy up a bit.

When I pointed over at Daniel, I expected him to be staring down at his phone. But instead, he nodded back at me with a goofy grin on his face. Whoa, I hadn't seen him smile like that since Year 6! What was going on? In that moment, my body was buzzing like the phone in his cool-kid pocket. Maybe my brother had my back after all! So did Mum and Dad and Grandpa George too. My football family were proud of me; they believed in me. I could do this! Suddenly, I knew exactly what to say: "Why do we all love football? Because we want to be HEROES, that's why! Well, today, you're going to go out there and do whatever it takes to become the HEROES you want to be!"

"YEAH!" cheered everyone, including you-know-who.

For the first ten minutes, my TOTALLY AWESOME HALF-TIME TEAM TALK worked a "tricker treat" as Grandpa George would say. Mo and Izzy fizzed around the field like they'd had a few too many fizzy drinks. Even Billy was boshing his way through to win the ball back for his team.

"Well done, William!" His mum clapped, wiping away a tear like it was a super-embarrassing bogey.

But just when it was all going so well, disaster struck. Tabs stretched out her left leg to make a tackle and...

"ARGHHHHHHHHH!" she cried out in agony.

It was bad news. Tabs had to hobble off and on came Alex C.

"Run your sock—" I started to say to him, but I stopped myself just in time. No more silly football phrases; just normal things that made sense. "Go out there and RUN, RUN, RUN!" I went for instead.

"Yes, Coach!"

Unfortunately, the bad news got worse. Much worse. With our best player off the pitch, Epic upped their game.

WARNING! They were starting to find bigger and

bigger gaps in the Tissbury defence.

DANGER! They were moving closer and closer to the Tissbury goal.

HUGE DANGER! As the Epic striker tried to chest the ball down on the edge of the area, Alex C charged in clumsily, hammer-head first.

He missed the ball and he missed the player too, but that's not what the referee saw. No, what he saw was the Epic striker:

1. Fall to the grass like he'd been hit in the face by one of Billy's boots.

2. Do four forward rolls in a row, all the way into the back of Gabby's goal!

In a gymnastics competition, he would have won a gold medal for that performance.

In the County Cup Final, he somehow won a free kick.

"No way!" Alex C argued. "I didn't touch him!"

"Ref, that boy's a DIVING, STINKING CHEAT!" Billy bellowed.

Suddenly, he didn't care if his mum could hear him or not, and for the first time ever, I was on Billy's side. I stormed over to Epic's coach.

"Surely you're not going to let your player get away with that? He dived and you know it!"

But she just shrugged and said, "Sorry, I'm not the referee, kid."

WHOA, who was she calling "kid"? Only Mum was allowed to get away with something like that.

Breathe, Johnny, breathe! To calm myself down, I updated my heroes list in my head. ~~Epic's Coach~~. So there!

If it had been a penalty, Gabby could have pranked that **SNOT-SNAKE** with one of her jokes. But instead, it was a free kick. I could hardly watch as the Epic striker stepped up to take it. I wish I'd buried my face in my extra-long scarf, but instead I watched as he curled the ball over Billy's and Alex C's heads, and over Gabby's outstretched arms too.

1–1.

It's really hard to describe that horrible moment, but I'll try. It felt like … like the Epic striker's shot had gone into my mouth and dropped down to the bottom of my tummy with an awful, sinking **PLOP!**

What now? I thought. I felt like giving up, but I couldn't; not when my family was there watching; not when my team needed me; and not when Billy was getting ready to **BASH!** anyone in his way.

Uh-oh. "TIME OUT!" I shouted, making the "T" with my hands like cool coaches (so not Epic's coach).

Billy was barking out his plan before he even reached the team huddle. "I say we hit those thud-heads hard and hurt them for real!"

"YEAH!" cheered Alex C.

"No!" I wasn't going to let Billy ruin our County Cup run now.

"Why not? They deserve it!"

"Because ... because FIGHTING'S FOR ...
FLAPJACKS!"

Billy snarled, trying to think of another reason. "OK, well, if they can dive and cheat their way to glory, then so can we!"

"YEAH!" cheered Alex C.

"No!" I said again.

"Why not?"

"Because ... because DIVING'S FOR ...
DINGBATS!"

"Wait, what's a dingbat?"

"I'm not sure, actually. I think it might be—"

Luckily, Tabs took over at that point. "It's a nasty name, OK? All you need to know is: WE DON'T WANT TO BE *DINGBATS!*"

"Whatever, I don't see you coming up with anything better, BALLY JUNIOR!" Billy snarled at me. "I thought you were meant to be full of great football ideas. So, go on then – what's YOUR plan?"

Think, Johnny, think!

CHAPTER 21

JOHNNY PLAYS BALL!

TISSBURY PRIMARY VS EPIC FOREST (PART III)

You know when you really want to wear your favourite Tissbury Town shirt (the one with 911 JEFFRIES on the back) and you frantically search all over your bedroom for it, making a total mess? That's a bit like what was going on in my brain right then.

We were drawing 1–1 in the County Cup Final, our best player was injured, our captain was furious and our Epic opponents were diving like dingbats. HELP!

What we needed was a master plan, and it was all up to me. What was I going to do? What

GREAT FOOTBALL IDEA, WHERE ARE YOU?

would Paul Porterfield do? I was even starting to wonder what Dad would do.

Think, Johnny, think! But no, I couldn't find my next great football idea ANYWHERE!

Uh-oh, Tissbury were in big trouble if I didn't think of something soon…

"My plan is … not quite ready yet," I admitted. "Look, let's go back out there and keep battling. It's still 1–1 – we can win this! When the time is right, I'll tell you what to do, OK?"

"No, you told me that last time!" Billy exploded. His big red face was about to burst. "I was right about you all along. You're a joke, Johnny Ball – you don't know what you're doing! Where are my old boots? I need them back. Come on, team, we're going to play this MY way!"

"YEAH!" cheered Alex C. He was still fuming after that free kick.

Surprise, surprise – Billy's plan didn't work very well. At all! He walked around bellowing lots of mean words, but he couldn't run fast enough to HOOF! the Epic players really hard. Instead, Alex C did his dirty work for him.

Push – *FWEEET!*

Shirt-pull – *FWEEET!*

Kick – *FWEEET!*

Hammer-head – *FWEEET!*

The whistle was blowing so often that it sounded like a song! After Alex C's tenth foul in two minutes, the referee came over to me.

"If you don't take that boy off, I'm going to send him off instead!"

"But, ref, we don't have any more subs…"

The rubbish referee just shrugged and said, "Sorry, I'm not the manager, kid."

"Kid" – argh, that word again. I hated it even more than Mr Mann and his silly football phrases!

Speaking of our former manager, it turned out that it was all his fault anyway. Had he bothered to read the County Cup rule book properly? Of course not! If he had done his job (like Epic's killer coach clearly had), then he would have known that, as the rubbish ref now told me:

"17.c) IN THE FINAL, TEAMS ARE ALLOWED TO INCLUDE A FOURTH SUBSTITUTE."

But it was way too late to do anything about it. Whether Alex C was taken off or sent off, Tissbury would still be down to four players. Unless…

Like all the very best friends, Tabia was thinking exactly what I was thinking. "Johnny, get out there and play ball!" she said. "You can be our fourth sub. We need you."

"But—"

"No. No buts – stop being such a **SWEET-CHILLI-CHICKEN**," she said, hobbling over to give me a good shake. "You're a good footballer, Johnny; you've just got to believe in yourself. Come on, do it for Tissbury!"

As always, Tabs was right. Our team needed five players, even if the fifth was me. Yes, I was a football manager now, but I could still kick it. It was time for me to play ball again!

"Can you look after this for me, please?" I said to Grandpa George, adding my scarf to the one already around his neck. I definitely didn't want that tripping me up on the pitch.

"It would be a plonking pleasure, miladdy. Go give them kittens!"

"And can you look after this for me, please?" I said to Mum, handing her my pocket notebook. I know I always go on about how super embarrassing she is, but she's super awesome, really. Please don't tell her

I said this, but I don't know what I'd do without her.

"YOU'VE GOT THIS, JOHNNY-LUVS!"

Dad patted me on the back and Daniel gave me a cool-kid nod. "Flame this final, bro!"

That sounded dangerous, but I'd do my best to win it for Tissbury.

As I ran onto the field, however, my adrenaline buzz faded away into … PANIC! I wasn't ready; I hadn't prepared for this. You know that nightmare where you turn up at school, but you've forgotten to put on ANY clothes? It felt a little bit like that. There was still one long minute left, and then extra time and penalties after that. What was I doing and, more importantly, what was I going to do?

Think, Johnny, think!

Could I come on and be Tissbury's Trojan Ball?
Maybe they wouldn't mark me because they
thought I was just the manager... No, even if
someone passed to me, Epic were never going to
fall for that trick twice in one game.

Besides, after Epic's diving, stinking cheating, I
had decided to change my style. From now on,
there would be:

NO MORE puking players,

NO MORE comedy keepers

and NO MORE Trojan Tabias.

NO MORE TRICKS!*

(*Well, sometimes maybe...)

Why not? Because TRICKS WERE FOR ... TRY-HARDS!

They might be all right for an assistant manager,
but not for a manager, and definitely not for "THE
NEXT PAUL PORTERFIELD", the future number one
football genius in the whole wide world. If we were
going to win the County Cup Final, we would win it
fair and square, with a proper football plan.

Think, Johnny, think!

The Epic players were grinning smugly, like they
had already won the County Cup. But they hadn't –

not yet! If they were feeling so confident, maybe we could catch them by surprise...

But how? Without Tabs, we were never going to out-pass or out-skill our opponents. No chance! There was one thing that we could beat anyone at, though – TEAMWORK! Tissbury had shown that against Bartley Moor and Upton Academy.

So, how could we use teamwork to win the County Cup Final too? Maybe with a TOTALLY AWESOME TEAM MOVE – something like the Lightning Bolt, only with a lot less passing...

TING! LIGHT-BULB MOMENT. At last! I rushed over to Mum; I was going to need my pocket notebook back. I scribbled down my master plan quickly and then ripped out the page and took it out onto the pitch.

"What is THAT?" Billy bellowed in the emergency team huddle.

"I call it ... THE FLYING T!" That didn't get the cheers I was expecting, so I started to explain. "T for Tissbury, duh..."

The next part I whispered because, as I told you before, if you've got a really clever plan, you should always whisper it.

"Right, let's PLAY BALL!" I shouted at the end.

"Hey, that's my line!" Billy shouted, but, for once, he had a big smile on his face. Here's another tip for you: if you want to make someone happy, just let them be the hero!

FWEEEET!

Gabby rolled the ball out to Izzy, our best dribbler now that Tabs was off the field. As she started to run forward, the rest of us formed a ferocious line of lions to protect her – me, then Mo, then Billy at the front.

"GET BACK, BOZOS!" Billy hollered and the Epic players were way too scared to argue. They had never seen teamwork like this – no one had.

"Keep going, keep going!"

Before we knew it, we were over the halfway line, then closing in on the Epic penalty area...

"When?" asked Izzy.

"Now?" asked Mo.

They were waiting for me to shout the magic word: "TISSBURY!"

In a flash, I made a run to the left and Mo made a run to the right. Together, we formed ... THE FLYING T!

The Epic players panicked. Who wouldn't? Our teamwork was terrifying! Two of them ran towards me – just in case I was another Trojan Tabia, I guess – and one ran towards Mo. That left one defender to deal with Izzy and Billy. Tissbury had a 2 vs 1 in the last minute of the County Cup Final...

Thank goodness Izzy wasn't a ball grog any more! Inside the penalty area, she passed to Billy and HOOF! he nearly knocked the goalposts down.

GOOOOOOOOAAAAAAALLLL!!!!!!!!!

TISSBURY 2, EPIC 1 – WE HAD WON THE COUNTY CUP!

You know that bit at the end of films sometimes, where everyone's running and hugging each other in slow motion and there's that dramatic music playing? Well, it felt a lot like that really. We were heroes now – in our school, our town and our county – and we'd never been so happy.

Suddenly, the pitch was invaded by an army of crazy, shouting people:

HURRAAAAAAAY! TISSBURY! TISSBURY! TISSBURY!

First to dive into the team bundle were Scott and Alex W, who were feeling fresh again after their nap,

then Alex C, who looked mighty relieved after his fouling spree,

then Tabia, who wasn't going to let a little injury get in the way of a good party,

then Mum,

then Billy's mum,

then Grandpa George,

then Dad (his right ankle, remember!),

then Miss Patel, the best teacher ever

and then ... Daniel!

Yes, even my cool-kid brother was jumping and **WHOOP**ing!

"Tidy tactics, bro! I knew you'd be better off

without Macho Mann. You can thank me later…"

Wait a second! "Daniel, what did you do?"

"I just gave him a quick call, bro," he said, with a cool-kid shrug. "Hyped to help. No big deal – I only told him what he wanted to hear!"

So, Mr Mann wasn't going to be the next Blether United manager after all – Daniel had made the whole thing up. Boy, Mum would ground him for a whole Tissbury Town season if she ever found out! But that wasn't what I was thinking about in that moment. What I was thinking about was:

"Wow, you did that for me?"

"Course, I've got your back, bro! Plus, I had to make it up to you, didn't I? After saying all those savage things."

"You're the best bro ever!"

After a quick cool-kid hug, I ran off to join my teammates again. Forget that hat-trick for the Tissbury Tiger Cubs; this was my new most glorious football achievement by miles! First, TISSBURY'S TROJAN TABIA and then THE FLYING T; I had saved the day, and I had done it in front of my whole football family.

The best day of my entire life was about to get even better too. During our County Cup celebrations, I had a hat-trick of visitors.

The first was Billy. He looked really uncomfortable, like he desperately needed to pee or something.

"Hey, I'm, err, sorry about what I said before."

Wait, what? Billy was saying sorry … TO ME? Was it because his mum was listening? No, she was on the other side of the pitch, dancing with my mum and dad. Weird in lots of ways!

"Tabs was right about you all along. JOHNNY BALL, YOU REALLY ARE A FOOTBALL GENIUS!"

Had those words really just come out of his

mouth? Had his brain been taken over by aliens or something? It was probably just the Cup Final glory speaking, but it was still a nice thing to hear.

"Thanks, great shot by the way!"

"I know, it was an absolute BANGER, one of my best..."

Phew, the old boasting Billy was back!

Then, a few minutes later, a mysterious-looking man walked over to me. He had his cap pulled down low over his eyes, like he was super famous or something. So, it was only when he got really close that I realized who he was.

"PAUL PORTERFIELD!"

I thought I had only thought it, but actually I had also said it out loud.

But he smiled and then said, "Johnny Ball!"

Whoa, how did the Tissbury Town manager (and probably the best manager in the whole wide world) know MY name? But he carried on speaking before I could ask that question.

"Congratulations, what a win! You've got a brilliant football brain, Johnny. If you play your cards right, you could be doing my job one day!"

Wait a minute – Johnny Ball: Future Tissbury

Town Manager? That was my number one football dream! And now that Paul Porterfield had said it, it had to come true...

After that, I didn't think my day could get any better, but as my hero walked away, Chris Crawley walked towards me. He was Daniel's coach for the Tissbury Tigers Under-15s.

"Well done, Johnny – you're a special talent! Your brother told me all about you and now I've seen it for myself. Listen, my assistant, Duncan Drills, has just taken the job as the new manager of Blether United..."

Poor Mr Mann!

"...which means that I'm looking for someone new. So, what do you think – are you up for it?"

Wait a minute – Johnny Ball: Tissbury Tigers Assistant Manager? Did Daniel know about this? I know we were now best bros again, but that would probably change pretty quickly if we started working together... Me coaching my big brother?

That sounded super awkward and super stressful, but there was no way I could say no.

"Y-yeah, I'd love to!"

"Great, I'll introduce you to the team at training next Wednesday. Six o'clock sharp – don't be late!"

MATCH REPORT 5   ✏ JNB

TISSBURY PRIMARY 2-1 EPIC FOREST

STARTING LINE-UP (MARKS OUT OF 10):
Gabby 10, Scotty 10, Billy 10, Tabby 10, Webby/"Koyo" 10

SUBS:
Clarky 10, Belly 10, Meddy/"Sicky" 10, Bally Jr 10!

SCORERS:
"Trojan" Tabby, Billy with a "BANGER"

A+

WHAT WENT WELL:
We WON the County Cup Final!

EVEN BETTER IF:
I was the new assistant manager of Tissbury Tigers. Oh wait, I am! Let's just hope Daniel doesn't mind...

Matt Oldfield loves football. He loves playing football, watching football, reading about football, but most of all, he loves writing about football for kids. With his brother, Tom, he has written the bestselling Ultimate Football Heroes series of playground to pitch biographies. Johnny Ball is his first fiction series.